MW01135011

A Beauty to His Beast: An Urban Werewolf Story

Natavia

SOUL PUBLICATIONS

SOUL Publications

Goon

Year 1860:

I woke up to the sound of screams and the smell of burning flesh. My mother and I were hidden underneath the bushes in the woods. She looked at me with worry in her eyes and I knew what that meant. My father wasn't coming back. He went to fetch us some water when the sun was out but now it was dawn.

"John, you have to be quiet!" my mother said in her broken English. John was my slave name given to me from Master Smith. My real name is Akua Dakari Uffe; I was born in West Africa.

The sounds of howling echoed throughout the woods and my mother hugged me close to her. We ran away from the plantation and have been gone for two days now. The smell of blood tickled my nose as the horrible screams and howls pierced my ears. Tears ran down my mother's face as she looked at me. "We have to go!" she said, grabbing my hand.

I walked on the tree branches barefoot as she pulled me through the woods. The sounds of howling got closer and the smell of blood grew stronger. The smell of burning flesh made my stomach turn as we headed closer to the direction it was coming from.

My eyes grew big as we hid behind the bushes. Hanging from the tree was my father. He howled as his skin burned—the smell made me cough then I threw up.

"Who's there?" a middle-aged Caucasian man called out.

"Right behind the bushes!" another Caucasian man shouted.

My mother let go of my hand as her arm cracked then it bent in a backwards position. Her ears grew out and they were pointy; as her body fell forward, she landed on her hands. The sound of her bones cracking caused the men to head towards the bushes with their shotguns and fire torches. Her teeth were sharp and her face grew long with hairs pricking out of her skin. I cried because I did not know what was happening. I backed away from her as her clothes spilt open into shreds. She let out a loud howl as she transformed into a wolf. She and my father had told me stories about the wolf-man and how we had wolf blood in us. I thought maybe that was part of a tribe ritual from the village they came from in Africa. My last name Uffe means "wolf man."

My mother's wolf was dark brown with a black stripe going down her back. She was massive in size. Her eyes were golden and her teeth were razor sharp. She looked at me then growled; I backed up against the tree. She leaped out of the bushes and the screams of horror made my heart stop. Something wet flew into my face and landed in my eyes. I touched my face and there was blood on my finger-tips. I peeked through the bushes and the beast that was once my mother was clawing at a disfigured body. A gun-shot rang out then she howled. Another one rang out then a few more followed.

Multiple bullets hit my mother, but she did not stop at-tacking the slave owners. Two more rang out then I heard a loud thump. I crawled further under the bush to get a better view and there she was lying on the ground panting and whimpering.

"Son of a bitch! Where in the hell did this thing come from?" a voice said.

"I don't know! But I think this is what's been eating those niggers!" someone else responded.

"This would make a nice coat!" they laughed not bothered that there were two disfigured men lying dead on the ground. But, they were used to death.

On the plantations, death was the norm. I saw it so much I was no longer afraid to see it. The beast that my mother turned into laid on the ground taking her last breath. The man with the shotgun pointed at her neck then pulled the trigger; her head was almost separated from her neck. A scream almost slipped from my mouth but I used my hand to muffle the noises. I did not want to be found; they'll whip me or sell me to another plantation for running away.

"Let's drag this beast back to the plantation. One of those niggers can skin it. My wife would love a nice coat!" the man spat. I sat and watched as they dragged my mother away.

When the coast was finally clear, I stepped out of the bushes. I must have fallen asleep because my father was gone from the tree he was hanging from. I did not hear anyone come back into the woods. The two men my mother killed were gone also.

I wandered into the woods for days looking for food and water. I was lost and could not find my way out of the woods. My feet bled and were swollen from walking on the prickly ground. I was dehydrated and weak. I had been walking in circles; my body collapsed as my feet gave up on me. I sat against a tree and whimpered. I was only ten years old and did not know how to survive on my own. I could not go back to my master because my punishment would be worse. I heard shuffling noises coming from the trees; I hurriedly hid behind one of them. After I hid, I didn't hear it again. I waited until I was certain that no one else was in the woods with me. It was quiet for what seemed like hours. I decided to head back in the direction I came from.

I walked and walked until I heard a stream nearby. Following the sounds, I came to a small lake that was hidden deep in the woods. I hurriedly stuck my face into the water, gulping and choking. It had been almost a week since I had food or water. I heard shuffling again then I lifted my head up. Across the lake was a wolf bigger than the one my mother turned into. I froze as his eyes bore into mine. He growled, showing his sharp teeth and its eyes were red. I backed away slowly with my eyes trained on his. I knew by its massive size that it was male. He stepped forward and held his nose up in the air as if sniffing something, perhaps sniffing me.

I looked down at my clothes realizing I still had blood on me. Before I could run, he sprinted across the water leaping like a gazelle. I fell face-forward when I tried to get away. I quickly turned around, but he was landing right in front of me. He growled with drool dripping onto the grass. I got up slowly backing up then he came forward. I closed my eyes as I prepared for him to eat me. Seconds later, I opened my eyes then gasped as a naked man stood in front of me. He was tall and muscular like an Egyptian warrior from the stories my mother told to me. His eyes were brown now and he had some kind of tribal markings on him. His skin was black like coal and his hair was in nappy long locks.

"What are you?" he asked me in clear English.

"I'm a person," I said to him.

"No, You are not. I can smell a human. You are not a human!" he said to me. I backed away from him.

"I don't know what you mean," my voice trembled.

"Goon," he said, laughing.

"What?" I asked.

"Goon, you are a silly boy. What are you doing roaming these woods? You are on the wrong territory don't you think?"

"I'm lost, sir," I said to him.

"You smell like an animal. What are you?" he asked, sniffing me as I cried.

"I don't know!" I said.

"How old are you?" he asked me.

"I think ten," I said to him.

"You are not a smart boy are yah? Or your master just wanted you to play stupid?"

"I don't understand," I said.

"You will during the next full moon!" he replied, walking away.

"Wait! I need food!" I begged.

"There is plenty of food in these woods, Goon," he said to me

"Why do you call me that?" I asked.

SOUL Publications

"Because, Boy. You are stupid! You don't know what you are," he spat.

"What am I?" I asked.

"You will see," he said, walking off.

"I lost my parents. I don't have anywhere to go, sir," I said to him.

"You have to figure it out. In human form you will never make it out of these woods alive," he said.

On the plantation, there were rumors of how runaway slaves and masters never made it out of the woods. I wiped my eyes as I plopped down on the ground. My feet had blisters and my ankles were bleeding from the thorns on the ground. My once light tan pants and white shirt were now brown and bloody.

"Do you have a master, too?" I asked him.

"Beasts are their own masters. That is why I call you silly. You don't know what you are and what you are capable of, Goon," he said to me. I did not understand what he was saying.

I looked to the end of the lake and there were two deer drinking water. The stranger's eyes traveled in the same direction as mine. His bones cracked and his neck snapped as he fell into a crouching position. It did not take as long for him to turn as it did for my mother. He stood in front of me big, massive, and hairy. He disappeared into the bushes leaving me behind.

I looked back down to the end of the lake and the deer were still there. Out of nowhere, the wolf leaped onto one of the deer's backs with its teeth tearing into its neck. The other deer ran off, disappearing further into the woods. The wolf pulled the deer through the bushes, and moments later the wolf was back in front of me with the deer still fighting to breathe. He clamped down onto the deer's neck, making a sickening crunching sound. I closed my eyes because the deer's flesh was exposed, blood everywhere.

"GOON!" a voice called out. I opened my eyes and the wolf was gone. He was in man form again.

"EAT!" he said to me.

"I can't eat that! It's not cooked," I said then he laughed.

"Dumb-ass house nigger! You are too fancy to eat this, huh? You are in the woods with nowhere to go. Now eat!" he said, digging into the deer's open neck, pulling out its bloody meat. My stomach started to growl and the stranger looked at me then smirked.

"Looks like you have a taste for it," he said, putting the bloody chunk into my hands. I stared at it for what seemed like forever. I did not want to eat it but I was starving.

"I just bite into it?" I asked him. He pulled the piece out of my hand then tossed it back into his mouth. He chewed on it then swallowed as blood dripped from his lips onto his chest.

"There is nothing like fresh meat. One day try the meat from a cow. Very good," he said.

Is that where all the livestock disappeared to? I asked myself. Five slaves were whipped, some even hung because many of the cows went missing.

I put the chunk inside my mouth then chewed it. It was tangy but better than the scraps they gave us back on the plantation. I chewed the meat surprised that my teeth were able to bite into the thick raw flesh. I swallowed it then wiped the blood from my mouth. I felt something hanging from my mouth and it was hard. I tried to pull it out but it wouldn't budge. It was my teeth: long, hard and sharp. I started to panic but the stranger smiled.

"First taste of blood brings out your beast. Your parents ran away, do you know why?" he asked.
"Our master was going to sell me to another plantation," I said then he laughed.

"Your intelligence level is very interesting. You are a white man's dog and when I say that I do mean literally.You do not know what you are and you don't know how to survive. You don't even know the reason they left their little home, do you?" he asked I didn't answer him.

"You are about to transform. First few years of transforming, you are uncontrollable. Your attitude changes and your appetite is out of control! The urge to kill for no reason becomes a habit. They didn't want their identity to be known especially with a young beast roaming around the plantation with all of them white folk," he said to me.

"I'm a wolf?"

"Yes, you are. Once you turn eighteen your aging process will start to slow down. We are immortal. These tribal markings appear when you reach eighteen. It burns like hell once they start etching through your skin. It hurts more than turning if you ask me," he said then left me alone in the woods.

For the next couple of days, my body temperature was high; I felt like I was getting the flu. My skin was sweaty and clammy and my heart started to beat faster than ever before. My gums were swollen, fingers stiff. I never left the lake. The stranger disappeared and never came back. I felt like I was dying, as I laid in the grass drenched in sweat. The wind blew the trees. I could tell by the whistle of the wind that it was going to be a chilly night but I wasn't cold. I felt like I'd been in the sun all day hanging up wet clothes on the clothesline.

The moonlight beamed down on the lake. The deer was still in the same spot; I had been eating on it for the past few days when my body allows me to eat. I cried out in pain as my back arched, cracking my spine. I screamed as all of the bones in my body started cracked and pulled. Sharp pains pierced through my skin. My clothes ripped off me as my body swelled and it seemed like I was ready to burst. The moon was now full and a small howl escaped my throat on its own. My body bent forward as my legs extended. My fingernails bled as my sharp nails grew out of them. My ears pulled the skin back on my face as they grew upwards.

I crawled to the edge of the lake to see what it was that I had become. I let out a wail as I looked at my reflection from the moonlight. I was not as big as my mother or the stranger; I was much smaller. My fur was the color of the midnight sky and my eyes were icy-blue.

"You are black as midnight!" a voice called out in my mind. I turned around then growled. There were four other

wolves standing behind him that were my size or a little bigger.

"You have a lot to learn, Goon," he said to me. He was in wolf form.

How could I hear him talk? I wondered.

"You still don't know anything, yet!" he said inside my head as he walked off. The others followed him then I trailed behind them as we headed further into the woods.

SOUL Publications

Kanya

Present Day…

I gyrated in the back seat of my friend Sasha's car to the rap music that was playing on the radio. We were leaving the club and were still partying. Adika passed me a blunt from the passenger's seat.

"Did you see that fine-ass man that was trying to talk to me?" Sasha asked us.

"Girl, did I? He was sexy as hell. He had big feet, too. You know what they say about big feet!" Adika laughed.

"Pull over. I need to pee!" I said to Sasha as we passed an old farm that was hidden inside the woods.

"Hell no, girl. This place is spooky as hell. You know this use to be an old slave plantation. One night supposedly some type of monster came through and slaughtered everyone," she said, laughing.

"There you go with that crazy shit again. Stop listening to them old folks talking down at the nursing home. They have dementia and all types of other illnesses. Keep on," Adika said to Sasha.

"Pull the hell over, Sasha. I'm about to piss on myself!" I shouted from the back seat.

"This bitch needs to stop drinking Patrón!" Adika mumbled.

I mushed her on the back of the head. "I heard that," I said. Sasha pulled over to the side of the road. I went inside of my purse grabbing a wet wipe. I opened the door then got out looking around, making sure that no cars were coming.

I walked into the woods behind a tree then lifted up my dress. I slid my panties down and squatted as low as I could to make sure I didn't get any pee splatter on me. I heard shuffling but I ignored it. It was probably Sasha or Adika also taking a squat. After I was done, I wiped myself then spat in the area I had peed. My mother always told me if I used the bathroom outside then make sure to spit on it so I wouldn't get a star on my eye. When I was done, I headed back in the direction I came from. I could still see the lights from Sasha's car ahead of me.

"OUCH, SHIT!" I said when I tripped over something. As I got up, I had something wet on my hands. I held them up into the light from Sasha's car and realized it was blood. I looked down on the ground where I fell and there was a mangled dead deer lying underneath a few tree branches.

I tried to run back to the car but I had on heels so I tripped once again, hitting my head on a tree stump. I needed to stay away from that Patrón! Every time I drink it, I always ended up falling. When I stood up, there was a figure standing next to a tree. I tried to squint my eyes to get a better look but his back was turned to me. It looked like he was trying to hide from me but I could see him. His skin was the color of nutmeg. His shoulders were broad and his back had weird tattoos covering them and he was tall. He had to be around six-foot-four and I could tell by his physique that he worked out. I gasped realizing he was naked. I got nervous then called out to Sasha and Adika. I was scared out of my mind! The next thing I knew, the figure leaped up into a tree and just like that, he was gone.

What the hell just happened? I needed to stop smoking because I was starting to hallucinate.

"Hurry the hell up, Kanya!" Sasha said, coming into the woods.
"I just saw something!" I said to her.

"What did you see?" Sasha asked.

"I saw this big ass man with tattoos all over his body. He jumped into the tree!" I said. She bent over and started laughing.
"Damn you, Kanya. I'm tired of your damn stories. Every time your ass drink or smoke you start seeing shit!" she said to me. I ignored her as I followed her out of the woods and back to her car. Perhaps she was right; maybe I was seeing things.

When I got back to the car, Adika turned the light on.

"Did your period come on? Where the hell did that blood come from?" she asked me.

"I fell on a mangled deer," I said, not believing what just happened to me.

"Maybe a coyote got to it. You know in the newspaper they said that Maryland had a few of them and one was even spotted tearing apart someone's cat," Adika said to me.

"I guess," I said as Sasha pulled off.

Adika and Sasha were laughing about something but I wasn't paying attention to them. Instead, I turned to look out the back window. I saw a big black hairy animal in the middle of the road. Its eyes were ice blue and they sparkled underneath the moonlight.

"Oh my god, guys look! There is a big ass coyote in the middle of the road!" I said to them. Adika turned around but it was gone.

"Drop this delusional bitch off at home!" Adika laughed.

"Fuck you. I saw something!" I said to them and they giggled.

Sasha dropped me off in front of my building. I lived in a studio apartment. I had been out on my own for a few years now. My parents called me every day, wanting me to come back home, but I needed my own space. After I took a shower, I put on my pajamas then threw my bloody dress in the trashcan before getting into bed. As I laid in my dark room, those blue eyes and tribal tattoos invaded my mind. Was I going crazy or did I really see what I think I saw?

Two days later...

The pay at the nursing home wasn't all that but it was better than nothing. Also, a few nights a week I worked as a bartender at a club to make ends meet. Sasha pushed Mrs. Carroll's wheelchair into the activity room. Sasha was average looking in a way; bone thin with stringy hair that she keeps in a ponytail. She is very light in complexion and is taller than I am; she stands at five-foot-eleven. I think she could be a model if she wanted to. She had the girl next-door look.

SOUL Publications

"GRRRRRR!" Sasha growled, teasing me about the animal I saw.

"Oh shut up, Sasha. There isn't a damn thing funny!" I spat.

"If you say so. So, anyways has Xavier asked you out yet?"

"What does Xavier want with my fat black ass?"

Xavier is the club owner's son that I work for part-time. He is Caucasian but Sasha swears up and down he is Italian. I don't know what his nationality is but I'm sure he isn't worried about me. Xavier is around my age, twenty-two. He hangs out with black boys and is somewhat hip but I still couldn't see him being interested in me.

"Who cares about that now a days? There is a lot of the swirl going on." Sasha said, brushing Mrs. Carroll's hair. After she was done, Sasha turned her back towards us.

"Help me!" Mrs. Carroll whispered to me. She didn't like Sasha because she said that Sasha was too loose acting and lazy. After I did my rounds and checked on the patients' rooms, I clocked out. I had to go straight to the club after just working a twelve-hour shift.

Once I got to the club, I headed to the employee's lounge to take a shower then got dressed in my tight-fitting, button-up black shirt and black skirt. Underneath my skirt, I wore black lace knee-highs with a pair of black pumps. I put my make-up on, giving myself the smoky eye effect. My hair was cut into a short cut with both of the sides shaved. I put my gold-hoop earrings in my ears that matched my gold bangles. I checked myself out in the mirror and was pleased with my look. I had always been chubby though I've tried many diets and exercising. I gave

SOUL Publications

up after losing only ten pounds and just accepted me for me. I was a size sixteen possibly an eighteen depending on the clothes I wear. I locked my items up in the locker then grabbed my tray. I headed onto the dance floor to get ready for a long night.

I made my rounds as rap music blared throughout the club. My feet were starting to hurt but I ignored them as I thought about how much I was going to make in tips tonight. It was overcrowded as usual since ladies were free before midnight. A table of men waved me over for drinks orders. There were about five of them and they all looked like they could be football players. Even though they weren't big and buff, they had nice arms and I could tell they were tall. *They must be some type of athletes.* They all were strikingly handsome with unique features.

"What can I get you all?" I screamed over the music. They all gave me their order, except for one. His head was down and he was on his cell-phone. He was dressed in a pair of jeans, Timbs and a nice button-up shirt. I could see that he had some type of tattoos on his hands but the lights in the club were dim so I couldn't make out what they were. Maybe he was in jail or something. I wondered if they were celebrating his release from prison, his aura screamed thug.

"Excuse me, sir! What can I get you?" I asked him as my feet painfully throbbed.

"GOON! Don't you hear the pretty woman talking to you?" the dark-skinned one who called me over said to him. Goon looked up from his cell-phone and I almost slipped. His slanted eyes pierced through me and his stare was menacing. He looked me up and down, a smirk formed along his full pretty lips. His skin was beautiful and his features reminded me of an Egyptian ruler. He was so handsome he looked like he belonged in another life, where only rulers and magical gods existed.

"I would like Henny on the rocks," he said. His voice tingled something inside of me making me rush off almost tripping. I heard them laughing at me and saying that I was clumsy; there was no way in hell I was going back to that table. I got another bartender to serve them their drinks. I went into the bathroom to splash water on my face. The burning desire to have sex had me aching between my legs. It had been a year since I'd had sex. But there was something about Goon that awakened every desire within me. When I walked out of the bathroom, I bumped into a hard, solid chest. I looked up noticing it was Goon looking at me with an annoyed expression on his face. He wrapped his arms around my waist to steady me from falling and the scent of his cologne burned my nose, further enhancing my desire for him.

"You are a very clumsy woman. Watch where you're going next time. You know you can't step on a man's butta's, baby," he said, referring to his Timbs. I pulled away from him and fixed my skirt.

"I'm sorry, sir." He looked only a few years older than me but his aura was very demanding. His presence was so strong it felt like everything was at a standstill and he was the only one in front of me.

"I'm not a sir." He chuckled. "How old do you think I am?"

"Maybe 100, who knows!" I joked, feeling shy.

"Close," he said jokingly, then his look got serious. "Next time just watch where you're going before you bump into someone that isn't as friendly to a beautiful face as I am," he said, walking away from me.

"What the fuck just happened?" I asked myself aloud. I hurriedly called Sasha and she picked up on the third ring.

"Yesssssss, darllinnggggg," Sasha answered the phone.
"I just saw a man that took my breath away! I swear he is the sexiest damn man I have ever laid eyes on. I think I need to get laid. Perhaps, a one-night stand? I don't know but I have an ache between my legs and damn it hurts," I said.

"Are you getting high again? Damn it, Kanya. I keep telling you to stop smoking that damn shit. Now you want some dick? What happened to your ass being celibate?"

"I'm not high, heffa! I'm just horny and it's finally hitting me. I went a whole year without the desire for sex and now the feeling won't go away."

"Is he cuter than Xavier?" she asked.

"Of course! What the hell kind of question is that?" I asked.

"So, this man you are talking about, how old is he and does he seem interested?"

"He looks to be no older than twenty-five. He has a nice body, he smells good, clean cut and he actually has a rugged mannish look. He looks like the type of man that will climb a tree."

"What is wrong with you and men in trees? Didn't you say that you saw Big Foot the other night in the woods and he leaped up into a tree? Girl, you have some major issues! Butttt, I'm okay with him already since he woke up old sally," she said, laughing.

After I hung up with Sasha, I made a few more rounds before it was finally time for the club to close as everyone was starting to leave. After I helped clean up, I headed out into the parking lot with my Crocs on because those heels were killing my feet. Once I got into my car, I put in my Jennifer Hudson CD then pulled off, heading straight home after a long day's work.

"Oh, just fucking great!" I said when I saw that my exit was shut down due to an accident. I had to make a detour using the back road. It was the same road where I saw that massive furry animal and naked man. I was too tired to take another way.

"I should make it home okay this time. I haven't been smoking or drinking so I shouldn't be imagining things," I said to myself. My phone buzzed on my lap. I looked down to grab it and saw that it was Sasha calling me. When I looked up, I screamed as my car swerved because there was a big deer in the road with huge antlers. My Ford Focus swerved into a ditch crashing head-on into a tree.

I groaned as I held my head. Blood was dripping from nose because my face hit the steering wheel before the airbags deployed. My windshield was shattered and the hood was bent up with smoke coming from it. I grabbed my purse and cell-phone then hurriedly climbed out of the car. My body hit the ground with a loud thud causing me to yelp in pain.

The woods were dark and it seemed like I was the only one outside. My head was throbbing and my nose felt like it was split in half. I pulled out my cell-phone to call for help.

"OOOHHHHHH NOOOOOOOO!" I cried as my battery went dead. I was now scared out of my mind. I stood up, limping towards the main road.

"GRRRRRRRRRRRR!" a growl came from behind me. I turned around and didn't see anything. I took off as fast as I could but it seemed as if my out-of-shape ass was still in the same spot. I heard shuffling noises as the bushes started to move.

"I have a gun and I will shoot your ass!" I said aloud. I heard more noises, this time from the side of me. I stepped backed until my back was up against the tree. I held on to my purse for dear life and cried.

"Please leave me the fuck alone!"

The bushes moved and those blue sparkly eyes stared at me. Its face was camouflaged in the night and the only thing I could see was its eyes and sharp white teeth. I trembled with fear as tears slid down my face when it howled. I was about to become its meal. There was nothing I could do because I was too injured to try to escape. As I slid down the tree onto the muddy ground with my knees bent up, I said a silent prayer as it howled again.

As I sat there its black paws stepped out of the bushes along with the rest of its body. Damn it was huge! It crept towards me and I could see its black bushy tail dragging the ground. The light from the moon and the stars shined upon us. It came closer to me, I closed my eyes as my body started to tremble. I heard the sounds of sniffing. I opened my eyes and would you believe it was sniffing between my damn legs.

"What the hell! Get the hell away from me!" I said, throwing a rock at it.

"If you want to eat me, go ahead! Damn it!" I said, picking up another rock and clocking it upside the head. It shook itself off then growled at me again.

"What the fuck are you? A big ass wolf? Oh my god, wolves run in packs! Are there more of you? I'm doomed!" I yelled and burst into tears. It came close to me again as its large body and tall legs stood over me. I looked up and it bent down, sniffed my neck and licked me causing its teeth to graze my skin sending a tingle of fear up my spine.

I closed my eyes as it sniffed between my legs again and whimpered. *Is this son of a bitch getting aroused?* I have officially lost my mind. There was no way I was stranded in the woods with a big, black-ass beast sniffing my pussy. I kicked it in the face and it took a step back. It paced back and forth growling and looking me at me like it wanted to eat me. I could tell by its structure and massive broad shoulders that it was a male, a strong beastly male. He was beautiful but very intimidating.

"Look, if you let me go, I'll go to Walmart to buy you the biggest cans of Alpo dog food. I am fat anyways and that won't be good for your diet. I'm too greasy and might just give you the shits. Damn it, I can't believe I'm talking to a damn dog!" I spat. Although my nose was bleeding and my head was hurting, it wasn't saying anything but for some reason I felt like it understood me. He walked up to me then sank his teeth into my leather jacket and tossed me up in the air causing me to crash down on its back. It jumped into a tree and carried me away. I screamed and cried because I was afraid of heights and didn't know where it might be taking me. I wondered if he was taking me to his family, so they could eat me.

It climbed up the tallest tree then leaped onto the next one. Its balance was good even with me on its back. I held on to its neck. He jumped from tree to tree until we landed out of the woods in front of a hospital. He got down on the ground then shifted me off his back. He then disappeared into the night. I know my friends would have me admitted if I told them what had just happened to me.

Goon

*H*er arousal still lingered in the air. I first smelled her when she was at the table getting our drink orders. When she walked off, I had to follow her. Her scent was sweet and strong, I almost shifted inside the club. I had just returned to Maryland a few months ago after being gone for over one-hundred years. The pack had been migrating across the world to different areas. Kofi is the name of the wolf who found me years ago when I was left in the woods. He was like my father figure and Izra, Elle, Dayo and Amadi, my pack brothers. We all have origins as far back as Ancient Egypt.

I was hunting when Kanya's car crashed into a tree. I know her name because I heard her friends call her that when she used the bathroom in the woods. I picked up her scent and followed her home that night. I have been with plenty of women, some wolf some human, but none of their scents ever made me want to shift as badly as hers did.

"Wake up, nigga!" Izra said, coming into my room. We lived in a mansion. Over the years, we collected a lot of things, expensive jewelry, rare diamonds, etc. Money was the least of our concerns while living the human life.

"What did I tell you about that word?" I asked Izra.

"I keep forgetting you was a slave," he chuckled.

"So, you sniffed the bartender's pussy?" I hated that he could see my visions sometimes. Izra is the youngest and can be very immature at times. He does things just for the hell of it. One day he shifted behind the grocery store then walked back into the store in wolf form to scare the hell out of all the customers.

"Get the fuck out of my room!" I said to him.

"Tell me what she smells like," he said.

"Like honey and strawberries," I told him.

"You took her to the hospital? Why didn't you bring her back here? We could've had fun with her," he said. I punched him and he slid across the floor falling through my bathroom door. I jumped on the ceiling and leaped into the bathroom landing with my foot on his throat.

"Watch your tongue, brother!" I said to him.

Elle ran into the room. "Got damn it, Goon! I just fixed that damn door! Why are you always fucking up the house?" he asked me. Elle was the oldest out of my pack brothers. He was the first one Kofi found and at times, he was like a father.

"That's because he has a temper problem. Now get your heavy ass foot off of me!" Izra said, pushing me off him.

"Keep talking shit!" I said to Izra.

"Goon is sexually frustrated. Look at him. All he needs is a hit of some good ol' wolf pussy to calm him down!" Izra said.

After they left my room, I took a shower. I got dressed in a Nike sweat suit and a pair of Air Max's. I could still remember a time when I didn't have any shoes and wore the rags my mother made for me. I hated when the era changed because I had to change with it, slang and all. I was aging very slowly. I was now one-hundred and sixty-five years old and didn't look a day over twenty-five. I changed my name so many times I often forgot I even had one. I still remember my real name but it's a secret. My name is the only thing I have left that reminds me of my mother. Not even my pack brothers know my name. Izra has tried to get inside my head to figure it out several times but I have blocked anyone from ever knowing. Whenever he tries to get inside my head, his nose starts to bleed.

My pack brothers all have tribal tattoos but mine were uniquely different. Once they reached, eighteen they got theirs and that was it but I was still getting them just not as often. I was a different kind of wolf and at times felt like I didn't belong. Kofi gave me the name of an old witch who could tell me who I am. She lives in Maryland and I was on my way to see her. I got inside my Suburban truck, headed towards my destination. As I was driving, thoughts of Kanya popped in my head and I wondered if she was okay. But then again, as feisty as she was, I was sure she was okay. When she wrecked her car her face didn't look too bad, she just had a slight limp and a bloody nose.

"Who are you here to see, sir?" the woman at the front desk asked me. I was at a place where old people lived and had people taking care of them.

"Mrs. Carroll," I said to her. That was the name Kofi told me to ask for.

"Damn, he is fine! I want to know how big his dick is. Maybe he isn't packing. A man that looks that good usually isn't blessed in that department," the lady at the front desk thought.

I chuckled to myself. When I first started hearing people's thoughts it drove me crazy because I didn't know how to control it. I used to hear people's thoughts all at once if I was surrounded by them but now I could focus only on what I wanted to hear.

"She is in room 317," she said to me.

"Thank you."

"He didn't look at my breasts and I just got them done! Huh, he must be gay!" she thought about me as I walked away.

My nose started to tingle and I knew that scent from anywhere. *Kanya is here!* And she is still aroused. I could still smell her wet sex. My teeth started to sharpen and my nails grew. I put my hands in my pockets. *This shit cannot be happening to me right now.* A howl almost escaped my throat but I kept my lips sealed. I could not make it to room 317 fast enough.

When I walked into her room, she was sitting in a rocking chair looking out of the window with some type of marbles in her hand. Mrs. Carroll looked to be only eighty years old but she was older than that. Kofi said she had been around for over a thousand years; she's from Egypt.

"Come and sit," she said as she turned her rocking chair to face me. A white old woman appeared in front of me then disappeared, her chair now empty. A figure appeared on the side of me and when I looked up it was an ebony beauty with long locks that stopped at her ankles. She wore a cheetah skirt and was topless but her locks covered her breasts. Her eyes were pure black and so were her lips. She had a lion's tooth pierced through each side of her cheeks.

"Don't worry. I have many disguises. Now, what can I do for you?" she asked, sitting on the table across from me.

"I want to know who I am."

"Akua Dakari Uffe! The son of a god," she said, sprinkling dust on the table.
"My father was a slave."

"Your father wasn't your father and your mother wasn't your mother. Although your slave mother carried you in her womb, you did not belong to her. The gods impregnated your spirit into her womb because she was a shifter that worshipped your father. You are the son of a god from Ancient Egypt. Your real father's name is Ammon. He was bitten by a werewolf while fetching water from the Nile River. He died from the bite as he bled to death. Your mother who is a witch practiced dark magic spells and cast a spell that brought your father back to life. She didn't realize the spell she practiced was actually a curse. Your father came back half man and half wolf," she said.

"You got to be shitting me!" I said to her. Suddenly, the door opened and the old witch disappeared. An old white woman was once again in front of me rocking back and forth in her chair. She looked at me and smiled.

"Mrs. Carroll, your dinner is ready!" a voice called out.

"Sasha, how many times do I have to tell you to knock? Where is Kanya?" Mrs. Carroll asked Sasha.

"Fine, I will go and get her," Sasha said, storming out of the door.

"I'm going to put a spell on that little bitch one day," Mrs. Carroll said. My nose tingled and my inner beast wanted to come out. Kanya was getting closer and closer.

"Maybe you should get spayed. You're almost to the point where you are ready to mate," Mrs. Carroll said to me.

"WHAT?" I asked her. I didn't think I was ready to mate or was I? None of my pack brothers had ever gotten their time to mate yet. Kofi hadn't even mated yet and he was the leader of the pack.

"Yes, Mrs. Carroll, what can I do for you?" Kanya's sweet voice spoke. I turned around facing her, she dropped the food tray.

"UMMMMM! I'm so sorry!" Kanya said, picking up the tray. Her face had a small bruise and her nose looked a little swollen but she did not look like she had been in an accident.

"You want to date my grandchild, don't you, child?" Mrs. Carroll asked Kanya. I growled at Carroll but only she heard me.

"Goon, this is Kanya; isn't she pleasantly plump? You know what they say about women like her, her body is made to be handled by a *beast*," Mrs. Carroll said with a hint of sarcasm.

Kanya blushed and looked away from me. Her scent was heavier than before and it was seeping from between her slit. She was wet for me; she wanted me to bury my length inside of her.

I'm so horny right now I can just rip his clothes off then shove his dick so far inside of me he would lose his mind! Kanya thought.

"It was nice seeing you," I said to Mrs. Carroll as I bent down to hug her. I sank my teeth into her ear then whispered,

"That's for being a bitch!"

She smiled and patted my back. "Call me later, sweetie!" she said as the wound on her ear healed.

"Just ask me out already!" Kanya screamed inside her head.

Sasha walked back into the room.

Lord, Jesus this man is too fucking sexy. How in the hell is he related to that old white evil bitch? He got to be adopted! Sasha thought.

"This is my adopted grandson, Goon," Mrs. Carroll said, reading Sasha's mind, too.

"I've heard that name before," Sasha said and Kanya elbowed her.

Kanya was right. He looks like a thug. Perhaps some-one who just got out of jail. She is better off with Xavier! Sasha thought. I wanted to bite a chunk out of her throat. It had been years since I last tasted human blood.

Who is Xavier? I thought to myself.

"Well, you all have a nice day," I said, walking out of the room.

Maybe, he doesn't find me attractive, Kanya thought sadly as I walked down the hall.

Later on, that night…

I sat on top of a building across from Kanya's building looking into her bedroom window. Her curtains were pulled back and a sheet was hanging off her meaty but-tocks.

"GOON!" she chanted as she turned and tossed around in her bed. She was thinking of me in her dreams.

"GOON!" she whined. I jumped from a building onto the top of hers. I climbed down the building wall landing onto her fire escape. I stuck my nail in the bottom of the window unlocking it. I slowly pushed the window open. She was in a deep sleep although she tossed and turned.

"GOON!" she whined again. I slid her covers down exposing her. I sniffed the air as her scent poured from be-tween her legs. I growled because I wanted to have her. She

pulled up her shirt exposing her swollen breasts. They were big and succulent enough to breast-feed a few pups. She squeezed her breast then she opened her legs putting her fingers between her pussy lips. She moaned as she called out my name. She wanted me to fuck her. I could see her dream...

Kanya was standing under the moonlight by the Nile River. She was wearing a gold skirt and a gold and blue armor bra. Her body sparkled with gold shimmers. Her hair was braided in long braids with gold beads at the end. When she turned around she swiftly walked over to me. Her hips swayed side to side. I could smell her sex; she was wet and hot. She wanted me to penetrate her as I read her mind. She reached out to me rubbing her hands up my chest as she stared me in the eyes. I bent down to kiss her, slipping my tongue into her mouth.

"Goon, make love to me!" she said. She laid in the sand, I climbed on top of her as if she was prey. My hands slid up her legs then into her wet soft spot, her back arched as my teeth sharpened. I ripped her clothes to shreds, as she laid naked underneath me. I licked her breast as my nails dug into her flesh; she was so aroused and turned on. The harder I licked her breast the wetter she got for my beast. My teeth sank gently into her nipple as I suckled. She moaned and I growled. I slid down her body lifting up her legs; a low growl escaped my throat as I nuzzled my nose into her pussy. I hungrily lapped up her sweet essence. A howl escaped my throat as my body tried to shift. I sucked on the pink nub between her fleshy folds; my nails grew sharp leaving scratch marks on her thighs. I nuzzled my nose further into her as I tasted her. Her moans were loud and her body shook from my tongue as it gave her pleasure.

SOUL Publications

A Beauty to His Beast: An Urban Werewolf Story   Natavia

"GOON!" she called out to me as she fed me from be-tween her thighs. I hungrily lapped up her flooding pussy as if I was drinking water from the river. My dick was drip-ping with wolf serum that was longing for me to impreg-nate her. The moonlight shined above us and it was a full moon. I turned her over and her round plump ass was sit-ting up in the air. She was giving herself to me; she was go-ing to have my pups and be my mate for life.

I spread her cheeks and placed my hardened dick in-side her. She let out a scream as my girth stretched her open. She was too tight for me. I slowly thrust in and out of her. My neck snapped as I fought to tame my beast. I would kill her if I had sex with her in wolf form. My teeth grew sharper, nails longer, and black shiny hairs pierced through my skin. I couldn't pull out of her! I bit her shoul-der drawing blood. The taste of her blood made me grow even more. She arched her back and my claws dug into her scalp as I pulled her hair. My thick tongue grazed her neck and her body shivered. I was a wolf still in man form. My ears grew pointy and sharp; my snout grew out more. I pushed into her causing her body to buck forward. She dripped onto the ground and her scent made me fuck her like a beast. I pushed her head down by the back of her neck. I howled to let the other wolves know that I was marking her. Although I might kill her, my body would not allow me pull away from her. My dick was stuck inside of her. Her nails dug into the sand as she made noises from pain and pleasure. I opened her up more, sliding further into her. I pumped faster and harder; my wolf serum burst into her giving her an intense orgasm. Her body violently shook from the serum I gave her. She was so wet that her juices dripped onto the sand making it moist underneath my knees. She had a mind-blowing orgasm, which caused her to scream...

SOUL Publications

I invaded her dream so I could feel her. I stood in the dark corner of her room, the pain and pleasure contorted her face. She had an orgasm in her sleep while I mind fucked her. She tossed and turned calling out my name. I did not kill her when I mated with her, which had me puzzled. The vision that I just had of her taking all of me seemed so real that it felt like it actually happened. I was drawn to her and had been since I first saw her. I knew that she could handle me shifting as I mated with her. How was that even possible when she was a human? How could a human survive my wolf serum? I quietly left back out of her window, disappearing into the woods. The vision I just had was overwhelming. Being sexually frustrated made me want to kill to satisfy my taste for blood. It did not matter one way or the other if it was animal blood or human.

Kanya

When I woke up, I was naked and my pussy throbbed. I had a wild dream that Goon and I were having sex in the sand by some river. I was dressed like Cleopatra and Goon was dressed like an Ancient Egyptian god. He even howled in the dream. He bit me like an animal causing me to have a mind-blowing orgasm. It felt so real, I could still feel his thick and long dick thrusting snuggly inside of me. I needed him! I was craving him, a complete stranger. My hormones had been jumping since the night I saw him at the club. As I got out of the bed, I fell onto the floor puzzled by what was happening to me.

"Damn it! My legs are numb!" I shouted. My body felt like I had sex with two men at the same time. My nipples ached and my breasts were swollen.

"What the fuck!" I screamed out. My breasts were sitting up like I had a major boob job. I crawled across the floor to the mirror by my door. I grabbed the knob on the door to pull my body up. When I stood up in the mirror, my hips were wider and my hair was in long skinny braids. I screamed as loud as I could.

"Who did this to me?" I cried out. I went into the bathroom to splash water on my face.

"Wake up, Kanya! Wake the fuck up!" I screamed out as I splashed more water on my face. *How did I manage to look the way I did in my dream?* I wondered.

When I looked in the mirror again, I was back to my normal self. I needed to see a psychiatrist. Since the night I saw that man in the woods, I felt like I was losing my mind. I even had a dream that gave me a real orgasm. After I took my shower, I put on a PINK sweat suit from Victoria Secret. I curled a couple of loose strands of my hair that sweated out in my Mohawk. I added nude lip-gloss to my lips and a pair of diamond-studded earrings to my ears. I looked myself over, satisfied with my look.

My doorbell rang, and when I opened the door it was my friend Adika. She and I had met in the ninth grade and had been thick as thieves ever since. I didn't get to see her much because she worked two jobs six days a week, so our time spent together was limited. Adika was also on the thicker side like myself. She wore her hair in a long weave and had the prettiest, darkest skin complexion I had ever seen. Her skin was so pretty, it almost looked like it glowed.

"Why do you look like you got some dick? You're glowing. Did you get some and didn't tell me about it?" she asked, walking into my apartment.

"No. However, I did have a dream about Goon. We had sex and it felt so real when I woke up; there was a big wet spot under my ass. Talk about a wet dream, damn!" I said, grabbing my purse and cell-phone.

"I have one of every time I watch Pornhub. So, this Goon person really must have you smitten. Everything has been Goon this and Goon that. What is he like?"

"He is such a mystery. I can't quite make out his attitude yet but his demeanor is very demanding. He has the most alluring eyes; all he has to do is look at you. God, why do I have it out for this man so much? I don't even

SOUL Publications

know anything about him. He might not be attracted to me," I replied.

"You are fabulous, Kanya. If he is not attracted to you then screw him. He doesn't know shit about dating a beautiful curvy woman," Adika said, snapping her fingers.

"His grandmother lives in the nursing home I work at. Maybe I will get the chance to see him again."

After I locked my door, we headed out to the parking lot. She and I were running errands today. I did not have a car yet because mine was totaled after hitting that tree in the woods. When we got to the rental car place, they were all out of rentals for a few days so Adika was taking me to the places I needed to go.

"KANYA!" a voice called out to me.

"What the fuck!" I said, looking around. The voice that was in my head was deep and sultry. It sounded as if it was from another time…maybe ancient with some type of accent.

"What's wrong with you now?" Adika asked.

"Someone called my name."

"Are you sure you didn't suffer a concussion when you fell that night in the woods? I swear you've been acting weird as shit since then. Kanya, you are starting to scare me. Are you sure you're fine?" she asked me with concern in her voice.

"Yes, I'm fine. I'm just tired that's all."

Truth is, I was not fine. I felt like I was losing my mind. Just a few nights ago, a big wolf carried me on its back while leaping through trees. How do you explain to someone that you think a wolf wants your goodies and how it sniffed you? Maryland wasn't even known to have wolves. Well, for now, I think I am going to keep everything to myself. I hooked up my seat belt then looked out of the window as Adika started up the car. A pair of icy-blue eyes stared at me from the bushes. I did not see its body but I knew those eyes from anywhere. They were the same eyes as the ones in my dream last night. Adika was talking about something but I blocked her out.

"Kanya!" the voice said in my head. His voice dripped with desire, he was craving me. My sex throbbed and my nipples hardened as a heat wave traveled over my body causing me to gush inside of my panties.

I put the window down. "Leave me the fuck alone you son of a bitch!" I yelled towards the bushes where the blue eyes stared at me from.

"Who are you talking to?" Adika asked, peeking around me to look out of my side of the window. When I looked back out of the window, it was gone.

"It follows me," I said to her.

"What follows you?"
"A wolf! It wants something from me. I am so scared. You should see it. It is big and black with blue eyes. It's a beautiful beast but its scowl is very menacing," I vented to her.

"I would never hurt you, Kanya!" the voice echoed inside of my head.

"DAMN IT, LEAVE ME ALONE!" I screamed, scaring Adika.

"Now, wait a minute, bitch! I love you, I really do! However, you got some exorcist shit going on with you and you are freaking me the hell out. You know I'm scared of everything," Adika chuckled.

"I'm sorry but no one believes me. I don't know what to do," I said with my eyes watering up.

"You can see a priest. You know they can pray over you," she seriously stated.

I rolled my eyes as I sat and thought about my dream. I could feel Goon's massive size penetrating me, his bites and scratches drew blood but the feeling was euphoric. When he pumped his semen inside of me, I had a very powerful orgasm. The orgasm was strong enough to stop me from breathing. I gasped for air as if I was drowning. His touch, his kisses, and the way he was almost animal-like was doing something to my body. Even though I had no idea what it was about him, he seemed so passionate in my dream. Some type of force was driving me crazy for him. I had two problems in my life! A big black wolf was stalking me and I was craving a man that I didn't even know. I felt in my heart they were linked together but how was that possible?

"I can still taste you!" the voice said in my head. I silently cursed it out until it went away.

A few hours later, we ended up at the grocery store after I ran all of my errands. Adika pushed a cart and I carried a small basket. I was hardly ever home, so I didn't need much groceries. All I wanted to do tonight was make a nice dinner for myself, have a glass of wine and just relax. I hoped that I could do that and have a peace of mind because lately I had not been able to. I was so lost in my thoughts that I bumped into someone.

"Oh my god! I'm so sorry!" I said, picking up their steaks.

When I stood up I almost dropped my basket; Goon was standing in front of me, staring me in the eyes. He wore a hoodie with a wife beater underneath and a pair of stonewashed jeans. He also had on a pair of Timbs with a baseball fitted cap on his head. I could see why Sasha thinks he is a thug because his appearance screams *"Bad Boy!"* He was so damn sexy, it was toxic.

He smirked at me. "I'm starting to think you like bumping into me. But I don't mind a beautiful woman like you doing so," he said, looking down at me. He was extremely tall. His six-foot-four-inch frame towered over my five-foot-four height.

I blushed, looking down at my feet. I dreamt about him last night and now I was shy around him all over again as if I didn't lust over him enough. Oh god, what is this man doing to me?

"What are you shy for? I don't bite unless you want me to," he said. He grabbed my basket from me. "I will carry this for you and we can get to know a little more about each other while we shop," he said to me.

"Okay, cool," I said, wanting to break out in a dance but I held my composure.

"There you are! I've been looking all over for you," Adika said, coming down the aisle. When she saw Goon her mouth dropped and Goon chuckled. I guess he was used to the affect he had on women.

"Adika, this is Goon. Goon, this is my friend Adika," I introduced them. He gave her the head nod as if he was saying what's up.
"Nice to meet you, Goon. I must say you are extremely handsome. You don't even look real," she said.

"I appreciate the compliment," he told her. Adika told me she would wait for me outside in the car, while Goon and I talked.

"Where are you from?"

"I'm from Africa, what about you?" he asked.

"I'm from Maryland but I have family from Africa as well. My mother is from West Africa. She moved over here when she was a very little girl with her parents. I have never been but I heard there are so many tribes over there. I would like to go one day but it's expensive."

"Africa is beautiful. It holds many stories. I go back twice a year sometimes more," he said.

"How old are you?" I asked.

"Twenty-four. I'm assuming you are twenty-two, right?"

"Yup. Easy guess," I said, giggling. "So, tell me, why do you have the name Goon? Doesn't that mean stupid person?" I asked.

"Yes, it does. I only kept the name because it was given to me during a time in my life when I was first learning myself. It's not the name I'm thrilled about, it's what took place for me to get it," he said, staring deeply into my eyes.

"I can understand that. Do you have any children?"

"Nope, no children and no woman. I am a free man. How about we finish this conversation over a nice dinner? What do you say? In fact, you can't tell me, 'no.' You've bumped into me twice and the first time you stepped on my butta Timbs," he said, making me laugh.

"Demanding, aren't you?"

"Wouldn't you want me to be?" he asked, gazing down at me. I shyly looked away. "How about tonight?" We exchanged numbers and I gave him my address. Our date was set for nine that night. That left me with about two hours to get ready. After he paid for my little bit of groceries, I told Goon I would see him in a few.

"What?" I asked Adika because she was staring at me with a smirk on her face once I got into her car.

"So, you are finally about to go out on a date. I can tell he likes you. He is very handsome too. No wonder you are trying to break your one-year celibacy," she said to me.

"No, I am not," I lied.

"We are human, so it's okay to want to fuck. Goon has major sex appeal. He reminds me of a felon," she said.

"Don't start that shit. Sasha said the same thing. Never judge a book by its cover," I replied.

"Oh no, I'm not complaining at all. Hell, I think that's what's sexy about him," Adika said, making me blush.

I was never into the bad boy type of men but there was something about Goon that had drawn me to him. After Adika dropped me off, I hurried into the house. I put my groceries away then ran me a nice hot bath. I added oil in the water and lit a few candles. I went into my closet to get out a nice outfit. It had been a while since I had been out on a date. I started panicking, I had to call Adika.

"Wear something simple. Do your make-up nicely and smell good. Wear a pair of jeans that make your ass looks bigger and hug your hips more," she answered the phone. Adika knows me all too well.

"You get on my nerves with that!" I laughed, turning my bath water off. Adika could've been a psychic because she had a way of knowing things. My lined beeped and I told Adika I would call her back.

When I clicked over it was Sasha.

"What's going?"

"Nothing much. I was wondering if you wanted to go to the club with me tonight?" she asked.

"I'm going out on a date," I said blushing.

A Beauty to His Beast: An Urban Werewolf Story   Natavia

"Xavier finally asked you out?"

"No, Sasha, what the hell is wrong with you? You like Xavier that much, maybe you should date him! I am going out with Goon. I ran into him today and he asked me out. And guess what? I'm going to go!" I spat.
"Okay, fine! Just make sure you carry some mace with you because he seems like a dangerous person. I just don't want to see you get hurt again.

A year ago, I was dating this person named Jason. He and I had been together since I was in the eleventh grade. One day we were supposed to go to Ocean City for a day, just to hang out. He called me early that morning saying that he was sick and could not go. I decided to take soup to his dorm room at the college he attended. When I got there, he and his roommate were having sex. Adika had been try-ing to tell me he was gay but I thought maybe he was just a pretty boy. He was what I considered metro sexual but he was into men. He finally broke down telling me that he could no longer fight the feeling and he was sorry for hurt-ing me. That was a year ago and I had not been with a man since.

"Let me worry about that. I will talk to you later." I said hanging up.

Sasha will never understand the attraction I have for Goon. There is something about him that I cannot ignore. Even if it was temporary, I still wanted to try it out to see what was there. I sat in the tub putting my bonnet on my head to keep my hair from getting wet. As I laid my head back to relax, that black wolf popped up into my mind. I was curious about it. I wondered why it followed me and why it did not kill me when I crashed my car into the woods. It took me to the emergency room instead. How can

A Beauty to His Beast: An Urban Werewolf Story   Natavia

an animal have that kind of instinct? Perhaps I was seeing things and the wolf really did not exist.

I had not heard that deep sultry voice in my head since earlier, maybe it was never in my head. As I relaxed, I put in my earpiece and went to my Pandora app. I closed my eyes to relax. I drifted off into a nap…

I was walking in the woods naked as the moon shined over a lake. The sounds of howling could be heard as the bushes ruffled. When I turned around, it was the black wolf. I walked to him, as my body burned with desire. I wanted him to have me under the full moon. I was sacrificing my-self to him. He growled before transforming into the body of a man. He was no longer hairy but he was black as midnight. He had a wolf's head with a man's body. He wore a big gold medallion around his neck. On his wrist, he wore thick gold bracelets. He held his hand out to me with long sharp nails that could puncture a hole right through me. I put my hand into his while my bodily fluids dripped from between my legs. He sniffed the air, inhaling the scent of my essence. I wanted him badly, that my body ached and my temperature rose as if I had a high fever.

"You are in heat." *His deep accent spoke to me inside my head again. He pulled me down onto the ground and slid his enormous shaft inside of me causing me to howl…*

I opened my eyes but I was still inside the tub. The sultry voice of Vivian Green had put me to sleep. I had another weird dream that made me throb. I whined from the pressure between my legs. I squeezed my breast, as I stuck my finger under the water, putting it inside of me. I threw my head back and pleasured myself as images of Goon sliding his thick, long hard shaft into my moist center went through my mind.

SOUL Publications

"GOON!" I moaned as my nipples ached.

My pussy clenched and warm thick liquid cum spilled out of me. My stomach cramped as I came. All I heard was the voice that was in my dream telling me that I was in heat. Didn't going in heat, mean getting pregnant? I was sure that term was used in reference to animals. Did that wolf think I was an animal? After I pleased myself, I drained the water out. I took a long cold shower to help the burning desire between my legs. After I dried off, I moisturized my body with shea butter before I started to get dressed. I put on a pair of black skinny stretch jeans with an army green camisole. Over my camisole, I wore an army green and black sweater that hugged my body, as much as my pants did and I put on a pair of black pumps. After I was done, I did my make-up and fixed my hair. Adika was right. I looked damn good! I sprayed myself with an African oil mist, which my mother sends me. It had a rich fruity smell to it. Goon would be arriving in twenty minutes. As I waited, I had a glass of wine to calm my nerves because I was both excited and nervous.

Fifteen minutes later, the doorbell rang.

"Oh god, he is here. He even came five minutes early." I panicked, fixing my hair in the mirror before sashaying over to the door. When I opened it, I almost fainted! Goon was dressed in a pair of jeans, a leather jacket with a black fitted T-shirt underneath and on his feet were a pair of black leather Timbs. He looked me up and down with his eyes lingering on my hips.

"DAMN!" he said, making me blush.

"I guess it's safe to take that as a compliment." I said to him, blushing. He grabbed my hand and turned me around.

"Where did all of that ass come from?" he asked.

"I see that you have a way with words, don't you?"

"Yeah, I say how I feel. I don't mean to offend you but you are sexy as hell. I will be on my best behavior and try not to act like a dog in heat," he said, making me laugh. I invited him in to offer him a glass of wine.
"You don't feel cramped in here?" he asked, looking around my small studio apartment.

"Nope, it's just me. How do you live since you are talking about my apartment?"

"Wild! I need room and space. A lot of space! I am not trying to offend you. I'm just a man with a lot going on," he said.

"Let me freshen up my face again then we can head out."

****

Twenty minutes later, we were on the road. The leather seats inside of Goon's Suburban were comfortable and spacious. Goon took me as a man who likes everything bigger, including his women.

"What's your real name?" I asked staring at the side of his face.

"Akua Dakari Uffe," he said.

SOUL Publications

"Wow, that's an interesting name and definitely different."

"Just so you know, your name means beautiful in the African language."

"Really?" I asked never knowing the meaning.

"Yes, and most definitely, you are very beautiful. Very unique. You were specially made when the gods thought of you."

"The gods? You mean God? We only have one and his son's name is Jesus Christ," I replied.

"Yea that's what I meant, although I believe that there is more than one type of god," he said. We pulled up to a fancy steak house and I was not expecting this five-star restaurant. They had the best steaks in town. I heard that an average dish cost over ninety bucks.

"We could've gone to Applebee's or something," I said and he gave me a menacing look.

"Kanya, if I couldn't afford it, I wouldn't be here. I like real steak not that bullshit they serve at Applebee's, now let's go eat," he said, getting out of the truck.

I shrugged my shoulders, Goon opened the passenger's side door for me. Even with heels on, he still towered over me by what seemed like over a foot. We had a reservation so we were seated immediately. I ordered a glass of wine and Goon ordered Henny on the rocks. We ate pan-seared scallops for an appetizer; well, I ate some because Goon's face did not look too pleased when he bit into it.

"What's the matter?" I asked, trying to hold my laugh in.

"This shit here tastes disgusting. I'm trying to swallow it but my stomach won't allow me to eat this."

"You are such a big baby. What kind of food do you like?"

"Meat, vegetables and fruit. I only eat red meat. It is good for your diet. Keeps you energetic," he said.

"So, you must have a four-pack?" I could tell under his clothes he had a nice body.

"I actually have an eight-pack." He laughed, showing his perfect white teeth.

"Tell me a little about yourself since you know about my jobs, considering I ran into you at both of them. What do you do for a living?"
"Nothing honestly. I was left a very big inheritance. Therefore, I do not work at the moment. Is that okay with you?" he asked.

I honestly didn't care if Goon worked at McDonald's. The attraction I had for him was beyond insane. Goon and I chatted, getting to know each other until our food was brought out. I ordered a steak, sweet potato and rice. Goon had a big steak as well that he wanted to be cooked rare. He also had steamed broccoli on his plate. When he cut into his steak, it was bloody on the inside, cooked on the outside only. My stomach growled as his plate looked better than mine.

He cut a piece then held his fork out. "It's very good," he said. I opened my mouth welcoming the thick juicy piece of steak.

"Ummmm, this is delicious!" I said as he fed me another piece.

A woman eyed us from the table on the side of us. She had been staring at Goon the entire time that we'd been seated. I looked at her and rolled my eyes.

"What's the matter?" he asked.

"That woman has been looking at you for a while since we've been here. I think that shit is rude. I could be your wife and she doesn't even care!" I said loud enough for her to hear.

"Even if I wasn't here with you, she would still be the least of my concern. Her scent reminds me of raw fish!" he said, almost making me spit my wine out. It was good to see that Goon had a silly side to him.

"You are silly!"

"Her scent isn't like yours," he replied.

"What's my scent?" I asked, staring into his eyes.

"Your scent smells like honey and fresh fruit. I'm sure your pussy tastes even better than how it smells," he said in a serious tone.

My floodgates opened and I hurriedly excused myself to go to the bathroom. When I got there, my panties were soaked. I trashed them before I freshened up. After I washed my hands, I went back out to the table. Goon had already paid for the tab. We exited out of the restaurant, our conversation was never-ending. We talked and laughed about almost everything on our way back to my apartment.

"I enjoyed myself tonight," I said to him when he walked me to my apartment door.

"I did, too. Hopefully, I will see you soon," he said, pushing his body further into mine.

I want to kiss him. I want him to take me right here and now! I don't want him to leave!

He must have read my mind because all of a sudden, I was lifted off the floor with my back against my door. Goon was holding me up from under my ass when he attacked my lips. I moaned as my breasts pressed against his hard chest.

"Please, just fuck me!" I screamed out. I don't remember unlocking the door or opening it up but we ended up on my bed. He tore my clothes off as I lay underneath him with just my bra on.

"I might hurt you," he said.

I wanted to slap his face! I needed something inside of me. I felt like I was possessed. I no longer knew who I was. I put his hand between my legs so he could feel my warmth. A low growl escaped from his throat,

"Please Goon it hurts!" I begged, spreading my legs further apart. He eyed my wet sex as a bead of sweat formed on his forehead. His face was etched with a painful expression from lust and his body temperature was hot.

SOUL Publications

I opened my vaginal lips for him so he could see my wetness pouring out of me. My nipples were hard and they ached terribly. I almost whined because it was so painful! The feeling between my legs was powerful and Goon was the only one who could help me. He bent down putting his face between my legs. His eyes stared into mine as his tongue slowly trailed between my wet slit. My back arched from what felt like a powerful force. He snatched my bra off, my breasts sprang out. His tongue was now hard as it entered me. I winced in pain as his nails dug into my thighs. The pain was so pleasurable.

"GOON!" I panted, holding his head between my legs. He looked into my eyes watching me watch him dipping his tongue into me. My wetness dripped from his lips and I had the urge to taste them. I had never been this imaginative when it came to sex until now. His teeth sank into my vaginal lips making me explode from an orgasm so powerful I almost lifted off the bed. He lightly growled then moaned, as his head moved side to side eating me out. I grinded my pussy onto his long tongue whimpering in pleasure. His hands squeezed my breast as he came up kissing my body. I reached for his belt unbuckling it, as I unbuttoned his jeans and slid them down, along with his boxer-briefs. I grabbed at his dick and it was enormous. I wasn't frightened like I should've been. I needed it and him now more than ever! I spread myself out for him so he could enter me and with my other hand I squeezed my aching breast.

"Are you sure I can come in?"

"Just put it in, please!" I moaned as my body burned.

SOUL Publications

My skin was clammy and tingled with a funny feeling. Maybe I was coming down with the flu. He held himself as he entered me; surprisingly I expanded to his size. I didn't think it would actually fit. My eyes rolled to the back of my head. As he pushed into me, the veins in his dick thickened. Was that even possible? I could feel every ridge of him making the feeling even more intense. We were connected in some way and I could feel it. Was he my soulmate? How was that possible and so soon? The lights flickered and the windows opened as he went deeper. Maybe I was imagining things. Smoke dust filled my apartment. An animal-like growl escaped his throat as he stroked me. I moaned loudly as I panted. My walls gripped him, causing his nails to pierce through my skin.

"Akua!" I screamed his real name as he grinded in and out of me. My hair grew in those braids again like in my dream. Blue eyes and sharp teeth stared at me. His dick grew bigger inside of me, making me scream, I was being ripped apart. But the feeling of it was making my body convulse. The smoke dust was so heavy that I couldn't make out his body, I could just feel his girth splitting me opened. My body lifted off the bed but I was so engrossed in him fucking me I didn't care that I was imagining things.

"ARRGGHHHHHHHHHHHHH,"I screamed. He pulled my braids, digging his nails into my scalp as he pumped harder. Every pump and thrust inside of me made me light headed, almost causing me to faint from the feeling. His dick pounding into me felt like magic. I saw Egyptian pyramids and dancing around the Nile River. I saw Goon and me mating at a ceremony in front of a pack of hairy beasts with eyes the color of rich jewels. I saw a vision of me giving birth and I could see this happening while we were having sex.

SOUL Publications

Goon

*K*anya's eyes were closed, as images of her in my life flashed in her mind. She was seeing glimpses of who I really was and although they were visions, they were real. The visions only confirmed that Kanya was destined to be with me. My nails dug into the ceiling, as her thick legs wrapped around me. I partially shifted and ended up climbing up the walls with her. She was hypnotized and wasn't aware of what was happening. She doesn't even know that my body is half-way in wolf form. Claw marks ran down the ceiling, as I continued to pump into her. I couldn't mate with her because the moon wasn't full but I did pump my semen into her as her nails dug into my back.

What the fuck? I thought to myself. Her nails were sharp too and her eyes changed color; they were gold. She scratched my back, drawing blood.

"Akua!" she chanted like she was under a spell. I leaped down from the ceiling placing her on the bed. She was hypnotized from my lovemaking. I shifted all the way into wolf form, bursting out of the window landing onto a car. The windows shattered and the alarm went off from my heavy beast. I ran towards the woods, trying to get further away from her before she returned to normal. I needed to hunt and taste blood. I had to figure out who and what Kanya really was. She wasn't just a human.

When I got back inside of Kanya's home, it was morning time. She was still naked with the sheet covering her lower body. She slept so peacefully. I put everything back on except for my shirt. I sat on her bed and kissed her lips. After I kissed her, her eyes fluttered as she yawned.

"I'm sorry, I was a whack lay," she said.

"Baby, you were far from it. You feel just like how I imagined but even better. Do you remember anything?"

"We made love then I went to sleep and had this dream that you were turning into something," she giggled. What she experienced wasn't a dream. I didn't want to tell her what I was yet but I'm sure she can sense something between us. She looked at the glass on the floor with a big hole in her window.

"What the fuck happened?" she asked, getting up.

"Some bad ass kids were playing football and it came right through the window. That's what woke me up."

She grabbed her robe then went to get a broom. Her doorbell rang, she told me to answer it. When I opened up the door it was her friend Sasha. She walked past me into the apartment.

"Oh my gosh, you are fine! I was worried about you when you didn't answer or return any of my calls or messages. I thought maybe something happened to you!" she said to Kanya while eyeing me. *I'm sure he has rape on his criminal record!* Sasha thought.

"Sorry, my phone died," Kanya blankly stated.

"Cut the bullshit! What the fuck is really up with you? Don't you see she is busy? Damn humans, some of you bitches are just fucked up," I said. Kanya's mouth dropped and so did Sasha's.

"GOON!" Kanya said to me.

"What? I'm not apologizing. Fuck her! Call me later," I said, grabbing my shirt and jacket. When I walked past Sasha I smelled her scent; she was aroused but her scent wouldn't even catch Izra and he fucks anything that walks.

"Wait, Goon don't leave!" Kanya called out and Sasha rolled her eyes.
"I'll be back. I have to use the phone," I said, walking towards the door.

"He better not be calling another woman!" I read Kanya's mind. I chuckled to myself. "I'm calling my brother!" I said before leaving out of her apartment. I pulled my cell-phone out of my pocket and dialed Mrs. Carroll's cell-phone number.

"Helllllooooo!"

"We need to talk!" I said.

"So, you want to know what Kanya is, huh?" she laughed.

"You know what she is?"

"Of course, I do. I know everything! It comes with a price though," she said.

"I'm assuming you want a broom? Tired of the wheel-chair?"

"Very funny. I will keep that in mind when I find a dog collar for you!" she said. When I heard Kanya's door open, I told Carroll I would see her soon. Sasha sashayed out in the hallway with her eyes trained on me.

"You are up to something," Sasha said.

"And you want something up in you but you couldn't offer me the biggest cow to fuck you. The dog in me won't even allow me to fetch that stick!" I said, walking out of her face.

"Skinny-bitch!" I mumbled to myself.

"Fucking asshole! I'm going to find out what you are up to! Damn hoodlum!" she called out to me. When I went back into Kanya's apartment, she was in the shower. I went into her bathroom and slid the shower curtain back. The soap suds ran down the crack of her plump backside.

"You want to join me?" she asked. I looked into her eyes and noticed they were golden-hazel. That wasn't her normal eye color.

"I'm hungry! Let's get something to eat!" she said to me.

I nodded my head then closed her shower curtain. I laid down on her bed looking up at the ceiling. There were long claw marks going across it and not all of them were mine. After Kanya was dressed we headed out. Her arousal was no longer there but it would come again and when it did, I wouldn't be able to control myself. I didn't want to attack her, but my beast and I weren't the same. The only thing we had in common was that we both wanted Kanya.

Two days later...

When I dropped Kanya off to work at the nursing home, I slipped into Mrs. Carroll's room. I dropped a vintage gold ruby necklace on her table. She smiled at me with her old white wrinkled face. She pushed her glasses up then wheeled herself to her small table that set by her bed. She inspected the necklace then smiled.

"This is back from the early 1800's! Do you know how much this is worth if you turn it in?" she asked me. We had a lot of jewelry from centuries ago. This piece didn't mean anything to me.

"Get to it," I said, sitting in a chair. She snapped her fingers then her door locked.

"That was very impressive!" I said then she gave me the finger.

"Kanya is a Jackal," she said.

"Keep playing with me and I will shift and eat your old ass! Is this one of your mind games?" I asked her. Witches are known for playing mind games.

"No! She's a Jackal! Very cunning and very beautiful!" she said to me. Jackals are like wolves but smaller, more like a coyote if you ask me. I'd been around for centuries and never saw a Jackal shifter.

"You mean to tell me my mate is a got-damn house dog?" I asked her.

"A jackal is a cross between a wolf and an Egyptian hunting dog. Shifters came from witch magic back then. But when they mated the offspring were born shifters. Your mother started it all with her spells! Jackal shifters protected the ground and hunted for food for the wolves. They were the last to eat after everyone. There was one Jackal that stood out! She was beautiful! She was all gold and the wolves couldn't resist her leaving the Alpha females angry. Her scent was undeniable! When the female Alphas casted her away, she ended up in West Africa where she mated with a human man. Kanya's ancestors are from West Africa. The beautiful one is the chosen one, the only one who can shift. Kanya is the chosen one from her ancestors. She is ready to mate, that's why she is changing! Only Alpha males can pick up her scent!" she said to me.

"Kofi is the Alpha of our pack," I replied.

"I just said that only Alpha males can pick up her scent, Goon," she repeated.

"One more question, since you haven't answered them all."

"This is going to cost you!" she said to me.

"You told me my spirit was sent into someone's womb and that's how I was born! That means I've lived before? Am I really from Ancient Egypt?" I asked her.

"Yes, it's called Afterlife. You were reincarnated. Those images you see are real. That was your life before. You have not mated yet, so therefore your life will keep recycling until you do!" she said.

"Then what happens after I mate?" I asked her.

"You will live for years, of course, until it's time for you to join your parents in the immortal world. You will know when they are ready for you," she said. I placed another piece of jewelry on the table for her then she smiled. When I walked out of Carroll's room, Kanya was standing at the front desk talking to a nurse. She excused herself then walked outside with me.

"Am I going to see you later?" Kanya asked me, standing by my truck.

"Oh god, he might think I'm too clingy already!" I read her mind. If only she knew we were meant for each other. What she was feeling was what she was supposed to feel.

"Of course, beautiful! Now all I need is my kiss then I will let you get back to work," I said to her.

As Sasha pulled up next to my truck, I grabbed Kanya underneath her ass picking her up. Once she was face to face with me, I licked her lips then pulled her bottom lip into my mouth. I sucked on her lip then gently bit it, as I squeezed her ass more. Kanya moaned and I could smell her wetness seeping from between that slit that brings out my beast. My temperature rose then I put her down because my body felt like shifting. Sasha eyed us getting aroused, I smiled at her.

"Call me when you get off," I said to Kanya. She waved goodbye then waved at Sasha on her way back into the building. Sasha got out of her car slamming the door and rolling her eyes at me. I looked at her then chuckled as I got into my truck.

SOUL Publications

Xavier

I roamed through the crowd of my father's nightclub. I went into the bar area and there she was Kanya… She is beautiful and was in heat. I always had a thing for her but when I smelled her scent a few hours ago I almost shifted. I'm a werewolf from Northern America. My father is getting old, so now I'm the new Alpha male of my pack. I'm supposed to mate with Amilia, one of the other bartenders that works at my father's nightclub. Amilia and I are arranged to mate because our fathers thought it would be best for us but I wasn't into her like that. Kanya's scent was much more appealing to me! Kanya's scent lingered throughout the club. She wasn't a werewolf, though, because if she was I would've been picked up on her scent. She was something else and I could only tell that because of the affect her arousal had on me. She looked at me then smiled; Amilia looked at me looking at Kanya then she looked at me and frowned.

"Why are you always eyeing her?" Amilia asked when she came over to me.

"What are you talking about?"

"I'm talking about you always looking at her! What do you see in that human?" Amilia asked. Amilia was a Latin beauty, and drew a lot of attention from the wolf pack. My pack brothers were smitten by her; I was the only one who wasn't.

SOUL Publications

"Get to work, Amilia!" I said to her. Amilia stormed away but I didn't care if she was upset. I walked over to Kanya and her scent was even stronger. A low growl escaped my throat.

"Hey, Xavier! I haven't been seeing you or your dad lately," she said, smiling.

"We were on vacation in the mountains. Really lovely," I said to her.

"I heard there are black bears in West Virginia. Did you see any?" she asked me.

"I saw a few," I said, eyeing her lustfully. Her hips were full and round, her breasts, nice and plump. She was made to breed! She placed a few drinks on her tray from off the bar then disappeared into the crowd. I went up to the third level to keep my eyes on her.

A few hours later, the club was closing. The staff cleaned up then grabbed their belongings to head out. Kanya was the last one out.

"Do you need a ride?" I asked her, aware that she no longer had a car.

"No, someone is picking me up," she answered, checking her phone.

I tried to read her mind but it was blocked. I could read her mind at first and when I talked to her, her mind was always somewhere else. She mentioned that I was very attractive and she also thought that she wasn't my type. When I figured out that's why she was brushing me off, I started to show her that I really liked her, but she never budged. Now, I could not read what was going on in her head.

"Let me walk you out," I said to her.

"Okay, cool," she replied.

We stood outside and made small talk until Amilia walked out with jealousy in her eyes. I continued to talk to Kanya, ignoring Amilia's presence.

"Ummmmm, Xavier do you not see me standing here?" Amilia asked me. Kanya turned her head then her eyes focused on a black truck that was pulling up in the parking lot. The driver stepped out and I smelled him; he was a wolf! Different packs do not bother each other unless one pack steps on another pack's territory and he was on mine.

"Hey, Xavier, this is Goon. Goon, this is Xavier!" Kanya said, introducing us. Amilia smelled him, too, and a low growl escaped her throat.

Goon smirked. "What's up?" he asked, sounding like a thug.

"Get in the truck, Kanya, let me holla at Xavier real quick," he said to her.

Obediently, she accepted his request. Once she got into the truck, he looked at me and Amilia. There were still some people in the parking lot and I didn't want to shift, but this arrogant asshole was tempting me.

"Scent smells sweet, don't it?" he asked me then his eyes turned ice blue. I had never seen a wolf's eyes that color!

"I will stay off your territory but stay the fuck away from mine," he said in a threatening tone. No wonder I couldn't read Kanya's thoughts. Goon had sex with her! He marked her! He was going to mate with her! After he threatened me, he got into his truck then pulled off.

"His pack was in the club when you and the pack were on vacation. He met her here," Amilia finally said to me.

"And you didn't fucking tell me?" I asked, yelling at her. She was supposed to make claim on our territory. But then I remembered that the claims aren't honored if the Alpha male isn't present.

"I didn't tell you because I was hoping he hooked up with her. You should've seen when she first saw him. She was very intrigued by him. I'm glad she is so you can stay the fuck away from her!" Amilia said. I slapped her face. She felt her cheek then looked at her fingertips. There was blood on them. She had three long claw marks going down her cheek.

"You son of a bitch!" she screamed.

"Oh, shut up! Once you shift, it will disappear," I said to her.

A hour later...

I paced back and forth at my father's house with my pack looking at me.

"So we have another pack in the area, huh? He came on our territory?" Aki asked me.

"Yes, he did! On our fucking territory! He threatened my life! I have to get rid of him. He is a dangerous wolf and I can see that he will be a problem with the humans as well," I told Aki.

"Call Sasha up and arrange something. I have to get close to Kanya. She is not all human. I don't know what she is but I plan to find out. I doubt if that arrogant son-of-a-bitch lets her come back to the club to work," I told Aki. Aki had been dating Sasha for about a month now. He was my only hope for getting closer to Kanya.

Lance shook his head and so did Dash. "Is there a problem?" I asked my other two pack brothers.

"You and Amilia are supposed to mate for life! Why do we have to beef with another pack? All over some woman? It's clear that she belongs to him. You said it your-self that he marked her!" Dash spoke up.

Dash and I bumped heads a lot. He always wanted things his way and he always wanted to be in charge.

"Do I look like one of those street boys that you hang out with? Don't speak on shit! I'm the Alpha in case you didn't know and quite frankly I'm tired of reminding you of that!" I said to Dash. He growled at me then stood up.

"Fuck you! You keep talking that shit! I don't give a damn who you are! Alpha is just a position, nigga! It doesn't mean you can't bleed like the rest of us!" Dash said, putting his fitted cap on his head. *That black son-of-a-bitch!* I thought to myself.

His eyes turned and his canines expanded from his gums. I chuckled because pack rules say he isn't allowed to touch me, even if he wanted to. Dash left out with Lance following behind him. I didn't care for neither one of them! But because we were wolves and this is our territory, we have to form a bond, that's the tradition and it has been for centuries.

My father came down the stairs smoking a cigar. He was four-hundred years old and didn't look a day over fifty. My father, Juan and I, are from Argentina. My mother was killed one-hundred years ago from a group of poachers when we migrated to Africa. We moved around a lot because we aged very slowly and we didn't want society to catch on to us. So, we lived in villages, jungles, deserts or just anywhere! When we would get to a different area, the Alpha male would have to face off with another Alpha male. Whomever wins gets to become the Alpha. When we first came to the area, my father was Alpha and he had faced off with Amilia's father. Amilia's father lost the fight and my father took over the territory, which later on was passed down to me. The two have become friends over the years—the defeated wolf can either join the pack or let the new Alpha run it or he can be banned from it and become a loner. But most wolves would rather join with the new Alpha because of food. They weren't allowed to hunt on a pack's territory, which is always the area that contains the most livestock.

"What are you ranting about, Xavier?" my father asked me.

"There is another wolf in town and I'm sure he is with a pack! This town is only big enough for one pack!" I said to him.

"It's big enough for more than one pack, son. As long as they don't hunt on our territory. We cannot go to war with another pack. Those can be deadly. It has to be a very good reason to start a war," he said to me.

"He came to our club! His pack was in our club, while we were on vacation! That is reason enough," I said to him.

"If an Alpha isn't present, a pack will not know if it belongs to another pack! Now, cut this shit out!" he warned me.

"Goon needs to go!" I said to him then his cigar dropped out of his mouth. All the blood drained from his face. I had never seen my father look so frightened.

"You can't mess with him! He is the son of Ammon! Ammon is our god! He is the creator of us all!" he said.

"How is that possible? Ammon ruled in 3,000 B.C! Goon should be in the immortal world by now!" I said to him.

"He has not mated yet, so he was reincarnated! He is very powerful! His mother is a witch. Because of her spells, that's how our family bloodline came to have werewolf in it. A lot of our ancestors migrated to Egypt so they could live for eternity. His parents are very powerful," he said.

"I don't believe in that! That's your god! That's who you worship! I have nothing to do with that! Goon is just a werewolf, like the rest of us!" I stated, turning around with

Aki following behind me. Aki and I had things to do and listening to my father rant was not one of them.

"His eyes are the color of the Nile River! He is the prince of the immortal world! Stay the fuck away from him! I saw him once in one of his lives and he is very powerful," my father said. I looked at Aki and fear settled in his eyes. *They have to be kidding me!* I said to myself.

"Well, tell Ammon to get his son and take him back to where he came from! There is no room for him here! I'm the leader of this pack and I have to protect them," I said with my back still facing my father as I headed out the door.

I took off my clothes leaving them on the steps in front of the house then shifted into my beast.

Aki followed me. *"Let's find out where they live!"* I said to him in his mind. We took off through the woods then I howled to alert the others that their Alpha was calling them.

I picked up Goon's scent from when he picked Kanya up from work. It took us two hours to find out where he lived but we found it. He lived in a mansion that was securely gated. Aki growled, pacing back and forth because we couldn't step on their actual land. As we continued to stalk their home from the woods, we heard something behind us.

"GGGRRRRRRRRRR!" a wolf growled. When I turned around, it was a big grey wolf with a tan streak going down his face. His eyes were gold and he was slightly bigger than us. He leaped towards me coming in full gear, teeth sinking into my neck, causing me to howl. Aki charged into the wolf clawing at his face. Fur flew everywhere as Aki and the other wolf tumbled into a tree knocking it over. The grey wolf landed on top of Aki and its teeth sank into Aki's neck. The grey wolf's eyes turned red, the color of rubies. I charged into him, piercing my teeth into his back. He shook me off him, sending me soaring through the air into a tree.

"What kind of wolf is this?" I asked myself. The grey wolf had tribal markings in its fur; I had never seen a marked wolf like this. Aki and the grey wolf rolled down a hill landing in a ditch. Aki howled out in pain. I could smell Aki's blood; the wolf was killing him. I ran then jumped into the ditch, biting the wolf's neck shaking him down, getting him off Aki. He clawed at my side, I heard the sounds of other wolves coming and I let the wolf go. Aki painfully crawled out of the ditch and so did I. Aki and I trotted away. I injured the grey wolf to slow him down. The grey wolf howled then more howls followed and I could hear his pack running through the woods to get to the injured wolf. They would kill Aki and me because it was just the two of us. We both retreated, so this was over for now!

Goon

*K*anya paced back and forth inside of her apartment cursing me out. "I have not known you long, not even a damn month yet! You think because we had sex I'm supposed to listen to you! You cannot stop me from working at the club!" she screamed at me. I sat on her couch flicking through the channels on her TV.

"Can you pour me a glass of water?" I asked her.

"Got damn it, Goon! Did you not hear what I said?" she asked.

"Of course, I heard you but I'm not listening. So, pour me a glass of water, please!" I said to her, chuckling. She stomped off to the kitchen then came back into the living room throwing the bottle at me while I watched TV. I caught the bottle with one hand never taking my eyes off the television.

"You are too weird!" Kanya said to me.

"We are weird together. You are not working at that club, Kanya. If you go there around Xavier's fruit cake-ass then I will be very angry. And when I get angry that beast comes out. When he comes out, I don't have no remorse! So, stay the fuck away from that club," I said to her.

"Get your crazy-ass out of my house!" she yelled at me.

SOUL Publications

I stood up, towering over her. "I'm going to let you cool off. I'll be back later," I said to her.

"This motherfucker is all types of crazy! I might have to call the cops on him!" she said when I read her mind.

I burst out into laughter then kissed her cheek. I patted her on the ass. "Keep it wet and warm for me, even in your dreams!" I told her. She slapped my face with her nails digging into my skin. I felt blood run down my face. I looked at her and she was very angry, her eyes were gold. I kissed her cheek then walked out; when I got into the hallway, my wound closed up on cheek. *"Feisty little Jackal!"* I said to myself, smirking. The more I was around her, the more her beast wanted to come out. It needed to come out and it needed to come out soon! I was ready to meet her. It was our destiny!

When I got into my truck, Elle's voice came into my head. *"Izra has been hurt!"* he said to me. I got back out then took off running through the woods that were located across from Kanya's building. The faster I ran, my clothes started tearing. When I finally shifted, I leaped up into a tree then sprinted all the way home.

I burst through the window to our home. Izra was sitting on the couch naked with claw marks on his neck. He was in a lot of pain, blood was everywhere! The pack cannot heal as fast as I can, it takes them a day or two depending on how bad they're hurt. So, for two days Izra would have to live in horrible pain. I shifted to human form and was now standing in front of them naked. We were all used to seeing each other this way.

"Who did this shit?" I asked them.

"Another pack," Amadi said. Kofi put some type of herbs on Izra's wounds. Izra howled out in pain; there were deep gashes all over Izra's body.

"What did you start, Goon? Why were those wolves sniffing around our damn house? Every time we find a place to stay, we have to move because of your temper! But this time we are not moving!" Dayo said to me. Dayo and I often bumped heads and had been since I joined the pack. We barely talked and when we did it was always arguing.

"Motherfucker, now is not the time for your stupid shit! You got a problem, we can take it outside but after I check up on my brother!" I said to Dayo.

"Everyone, get out!" I said to them.

I grabbed the towel Kofi was going to use to clean Izra's wounds. Elle and Amadi left the living room. Kofi looked at me then Dayo grilled me.

"You are not the Alpha! You don't bark orders!" Dayo said to me. Kofi shook his head.

"Let's just leave!" Kofi said to Dayo.

"You are supposed to be Alpha! Why does he always give the orders and you listen?" Dayo asked Kofi. I put the herbal drink up to Izra's lips so he could drink it.

"Not now, Dayo!" Kofi said, walking out of the living room. Dayo threw his hands up in frustration then followed Kofi.

"I fucked those niggas up!" Izra said in a whisper. His temperature was dropping and his lips were turning blue.

SOUL Publications

He was losing a lot of blood. I put a deep cut in my arm with my sharp nail then held it over Izra's cup, letting my blood drip into it. I poured the drink into his mouth and moments later he yelled as his wounds started to close up.

"ARGGGGGHHHHHHHHHHHHHHH! It burns!" he yelled as his skin pulled together.

Minutes later, his wounds were completely gone. My blood was what healed me faster than the other wolves and whomever else I gave it to. Izra and I were the only ones who knew about this. I also think that Kofi knows more about me than he leads on. Izra was attacked when we migrated back to Africa years ago by lions and it almost killed him. A strange voice came into my head telling me what to do. It was the voice of a woman and now that I know my mother was in the immortal world, I am for certain, that voice belonged to her. After I gave him my blood, he healed immediately after but that was something that stayed between him and I. We always joked and said we were blood brothers, not just pack brothers, and it was true.

"That shit hurt, nigga!" he said weakly. He still lost a lot of blood but he would be okay with plenty of rest and raw bloody meat.

"Shut the fuck up! You are living aren't you?" I asked, helping him up the stairs as the others looked on.

"His wounds are closed! What happened?" Elle asked me.

"Miracles!" I said then Izra and I burst into laughter.

Dayo got mad and walked out the door. Kofi patted Izra and I on our backs then headed towards his room. Elle and Amadi said they were going to sniff around the area to make sure the other wolves were gone.

"I think Dayo likes dick! That nigga is always acting like a damn yorkie! Bitch-ass nigga needs to wear a collar, so some motherfucker can throw his bougie ass some Beggin' Strips!" Izra fussed then I laughed.

"That's still our brother," I said, smirking.

"Yeah, whatever! Fuck that nigga!" Izra replied.

"How did you run into the other wolves?" I asked him.

"I was hunting. I was ready to catch this deer. She was nice and juicy, I think she was pregnant. She would've held me over for three days maybe four. But anyways, I smelled another scent then I heard growling. I followed the scent and it led me by our gate. They were watching our house!" Izra said as I helped him into his bed.

"It must be Xavier," I said to him.

"Who the fuck is that?" he asked me.

I told Izra everything I found out within the past couple of days. I told him about Kanya and how she and I are connected by fate. When I told him Kanya was a jackal he had a disappointed look on his face.

"Yo, you mean to tell me that all of this shit is over a jackal? A fucking jackal, Goon? Do you know how big you are when you shift? Do you know how small jackals are? My nigga, go back to that witch and tell that bitch you want your jewelry back because that information she gave you is inaccurate! I could've found you an Alaskan husky with blue eyes, if you wanted an exotic bitch!" Izra said. I tried to stifle my laugh but I burst into a fit of laughter. Usually Izra and I would shift then fight each other but he was still weak.

"I just gave you my blood and you throw salt on my mate like that? She is so beautiful! And she is feisty! She is the chosen one for me from the gods. It's in our roots that we mate who is chosen for us. Kanya's roots go back to Egypt and although her ancestors went to West Africa, she still has Egyptian roots. So, when you see your sister-in-law behave or I'm going to fuck you up! Even if you think about some shit that's foul, I'm fucking you up. Now, get some rest so I can knock your ass out when you get better," I said to Izra and he shook his head. I headed out of his room then he called out to me.

"What is her home-girl looking like? Does she have a fat ass? I know she got some friends!" he said to me.

"Adika is pretty! Sasha, her other friend's, pH balance is off though!" I said to him.

"What kind of off? Like she need to wash down there, type of off? Or is it a need medical treatment kind of off?" Izra asked.

Sometimes I hated that we were able to smell women without being intimate with them. Wolves didn't become aroused because of looks although that was a plus, we became aroused from a woman's scent.

"I'll holla at you tomorrow!" I said to Izra, ignoring him.

"About time you starting to get hip! You used to be like 'yes massa! No massa! I'z sorry!" Izra said, mimicking a slave.

"Fuck you! I been with it!" I said, slamming his door shut.

When I went into my room at the end of the hall, I headed straight to my bed. My bed was made bigger than a king-size bed and it was sturdier. I laid down across my bed with Kanya on my mind: her beautiful smile and her shy attitude. She was so full of life. I needed to tell her about us but that might frighten her. I had to figure out a way she could see for herself what she really is. I also needed to figure out what I was going to do about Xavier. He came to my home and that was against pack rules! The number one rule: Never step foot on another pack's homeland.

Kanya

I tossed and turned all night thinking about Goon. He was adamant that I stay away from the club but I needed my second job. My first job didn't pay much and with the cost of living in Maryland, I needed both jobs to make ends meet. I had no vehicle and the check they sent me for my car being totaled was going into my savings account. I got dressed in my scrubs after I got out of the shower. I grabbed my to-go cup of coffee off the counter and my bagel. I locked my apartment door then headed out of my building.

"I know this crazy asshole did not camp outside of my building!" I said out loud looking at Goon's truck in the parking lot. I couldn't see through the tinted windows but I was for certain he was in there.

I knocked on the passenger side door. "Are you stalking me?" I asked but I didn't get an answer as I continued to bang on his window.

"It's too early for this shit, Goon!" I shouted, walking around to the driver's side. The door on the driver's side was wide open and pieces of clothes were shredded on the ground leading to the woods. I dropped my coffee and bagel then hurriedly pulled out my cell-phone to call the police. Sasha was pulling up to my building to pick me up for work.

"What's going on?" she asked, getting out of her car. Tears fell from my eyes and my hands shook while I talked to the operator.

SOUL Publications

Ten minutes later...

"Ma'am, calm down and tell me what happened. We can't find your friend if you don't cooperate," the African-American male officer said to me.

"There has been a big wolf following me! He stalked me a few days ago when I was on my way to the grocery store! I also saw it when I crashed my car in the woods! I think he took my friend and ate him!" I said to the officers.

"This shit is so fucking embarrassing," Sasha mumbled.

"Now, you say you two got into an argument then he left? His vehicle is here and pieces of clothing are scattered around. Are there any crazy ex-boyfriends hanging around? Perhaps there was some type of scuffle going on?" the Caucasian female officer asked me.

"Damn it! I just told you two we argued because he wanted me to quit my job! He left my apartment and this morning, I came out and found his truck here! The black wolf got him! What don't you two understand?" I asked them.

They looked at me as if I was going crazy and Sasha started whistling looking around; a few of my neighbors watched me yell and scream with tears coming down my face. After they listened to me, they suggested I needed help and should see someone then the officers left. They didn't even write down my statement! All they said was give him twenty-four hours before I could report him missing. I shut Goon's truck door then locked it just in case someone wanted to steal something out of his truck. When

I got into Sasha's car, I burst into tears. I was losing my mind! Since the moment I'd met Goon, I had not been the same. Now I was going crazy thinking that something happened to him. I believed that wolf got him but nobody else believed me!

"I think your ex-boyfriend screwed your head up, Kanya. I also think you and Goon are moving too fast. It's only been a week and you two have been inseparable. Okay, I get it, the dick is amazing like you said it was. But damn, Kanya, get out of his ass! He probably has a wife and she might've caught him coming out of your apartment. She probably cut his ass up then dragged him home," Sasha said to me.

"You don't understand, Sasha. I think I love him," I said to her almost causing her to swerve off the road. Horns honked as she slammed on the brakes when she got in the emergency lane.

"Have you lost your mind? You don't know him! How in the hell do you love him?" she asked me.

"I feel it in my soul. I don't know why but it feels like I'm supposed to. I feel like he and I belong together! I can still feel his hands on me. I dream about him. He and I are connected. What's wrong with me? Why does he have a hold on me already?" I rhetorically asked her.

"Is the sex really that good? I'm going to pretend that we didn't have this conversation. Love? Fucking love, Kanya?" Sasha asked me.

While at work, I was constantly calling Goon's cellphone and all it did was ring. I sent him text messages back-to-back and still no response. I took Mrs. Carroll her lunch because Sasha refused to take it to her. My mind was all over the place! I should've come to Mrs. Carroll about Goon as soon as I came into work. I walked into her room and she was chanting something.

"Mrs. Carroll, have you talked to Goon?" I asked, sitting her tray down.

"Well, yes I have! He said you wanted your space and he's going to give it to you," she said to me. *I cannot believe that jackass!* I thought to myself.

"He left his truck in front of my building and there were shredded clothes everywhere! What was the purpose of that?" I asked his grandmother.

"Maybe he needed to run and blow off some steam. He has always been very animated," she spat. She lifted the cover lid on her tray then frowned her nose up.

"What the hell is this? It looks like I need to stab it!" she said, poking the mystery meat on her plate.

"Well, since I know he is alright, I will be going. Buzz me, when you are finished with your tray," I said, leaving her room.

I was relieved after talking to Mrs. Carroll. Once my shift was over, I clocked out. I called a cab then waited outside of the nursing home for it. Sasha said she would take me home but I didn't want to be bothered. I just wanted to take a nice warm bath, then go to sleep.

After I paid the cab driver, I got out, walked into my building then up the four flights of stairs. Goon was standing by my door looking at me with his bedroom eyes. He had on a jogging sweat suit but I could still make out his muscular frame underneath it. I was excited to see him but I didn't want to show it. I was still mad at him for having me worried about him.

"You pissed me off," I said to him.

"We need to talk," he replied as I unlocked my apartment door.

When we walked inside of my apartment, I slammed my purse down on the couch then crossed my arms.

"I was worried about you! I thought a wolf took you in the woods and ate you! Don't do that again!" I yelled at him.

"Are you done yelling at me, Kanya?" he asked, walking closer to me. I rolled my eyes at him when he grabbed me. He pulled me to the mirror by the door then got behind me.

"What are you doing?" I asked him.

"I'm showing you who we are. It's hard to explain but seeing for yourself will be easier," he said to me.

He pulled my pants down then ripped my panties off. He ripped my scrub top off then my bra. I stood naked in the mirror with Goon standing behind me. He took off his clothes and we stood there naked. As he stood behind me, he groped my breasts then squeezed my nipples, slightly pinching them. My pussy throbbed as my opening let out a stream of my essence. Goon growled then squeezed my breasts harder. He placed kisses on my neck then licked behind my ear. I moaned as his hands worked magic over my body. Every time Goon touched me, I felt like I was under a spell. He made me turn into another person, a person that needed him, wanted him and lustfully desired him. My essence dripped down my legs then spilled onto the carpet. Goon inhaled my scent sniffing the air with his dick pressed against my ass cheeks.

"Goon! Please take me!" I begged him. He grabbed me by the back of my neck then pushed me forward, arching my back.

"Look at me in the mirror! Whatever you see, don't take your eyes off of us," he said, kneeling down.

My palms were against the mirror, as Goon's hands roamed my body as if he was frisk searching me. He spread my legs wider then opened my vaginal lips. His nails dug into my ass checks, tongue slipping into my clenching hole, causing me to yell out. He massaged my ass as his tongue went in and out of me. He growled loudly making me wetter. His thick tongue pulled out of me then went up and down my slit then across my clit in a slow snake-like motion.

"OHHHHHHHHHHHH!" I moaned as my legs shook.

Goon's tongue entered me again, this time going further into me. I reached down between my legs to open my lips wider for him; I wanted to feed him my essence. His head thrashed around as his tongue touched places inside of me that it shouldn't have. My pussy gripped his tongue; he pulled it out then sucked on my swollen bud. I started squirting as he lapped up everything that poured out of me. When he stood up, my heart almost stopped as I looked at him in the mirror. His eyes were blue, teeth long and sharp. He grabbed my breast and his nails scratched my skin.

SOUL Publications

"WHAT THE HELL!" I screamed.

My voice went silent when he plunged into me. He reached his hand around me then gripped my throat as he kissed my neck, then my shoulder as he lightly choked me. His tongue circled around my neck; he sank his teeth so far into my flesh that I screamed. His dick went deeper inside of me, as tears fell from my eyes from the pain and pleasure that his huge dick was giving me. He growled in my ear then a growl escaped my throat. My nails grew out gold and sharp. My eyes turned gold then my teeth grew out making my gums feel like they had a knife going through them. Goon went further into me; his size grew with his ears sharpening. His face grew out, resembling the half-man, half-wolf I dreamt about a few days ago. His body turned black as midnight and that is when I realized he was the beast that had been haunting me. I tried to scream but I couldn't because my body shook with so much pleasure. Tiny hairs pierced through my skin feeling like needles—it was gold hair. My face grew out almost resembling a wolf's, as my eyes slanted more. My back cracked as Goon slammed into me with his member hitting my spine pleasurably. I fell forward onto the floor. I was in pain! The sounds that came from me were that of an animal. When I looked up, Goon was in wolf form staring at me.

"You are turning! I'm sorry for hurting you but biting you was the only way!" he said in my head.

"Goon, it hurts! Why did you do this to me?" I asked him.

"You were already immortal! You just needed me to make your beast come out! Only your mate can make your beast come out!" he said to me.

SOUL Publications

I whimpered as my body turned into an animal's. When I looked in the mirror, I was looking at a wolf. My fur was gold and so were my eyes; I was a golden wolf. Goon stood behind me, his wolf towered over mine. He was huge in size, bigger than a lion, and his icy-blue eyes stared at me.

"You are beautiful!" he said to me.

I turned around then attacked him. He howled out in pain as my teeth sank into his neck. I was angry and I could not control myself. He gently slung me off him then charged through the board I had over my window. He landed on the sidewalk and took off through the woods. I chased after him; my vision was better, my ears were sensitive and I could smell him. Goon's wolf was faster than mine but I was not far behind. I bit his hind leg and he howled.

"Damn, your teeth are sharp!" he said inside my mind.

He shook me off him then leaped up into a tree. I followed him, going from tree to tree until he landed by a gate where a mansion sat behind it. He jumped over the gate and I followed behind him. He ran up to the door and a young man opened it for him. The person looked at Goon then looked at me. I realized he was one of the people that was at the club with Goon when I first saw him.

"That's Kanya?" he asked Goon. Goon shifted back to human form and was now standing in front of us naked!

"Yes, this is Kanya. Where is everyone else?" he asked the person.

"Hunting," he answered him. I yelped out in pain as my body started to feel different.

"Go grab a blanket, Izra. She's ready to shift back," Goon told him.

He ran down the hall then came back with a blanket. Goon kneeled down then covered my body. I was in a fetal position when my body went back to human form.

"You son-of- a- bitch! You fucking did this to me!" I said, clocking him in the eye.

"Damn, Goon she's feisty! What's up, bartender?" Izra asked me. I rolled my eyes at him, as I stood up on wobbly legs. The blanket covered most of my naked body. I got a good look at Izra. He was boyishly handsome! His skin was the color of pecans; his eyes were the shape of almonds. He was shorter than Goon by a few inches and was a little slimmer. His cheekbones were high, his teeth snow white; he even had dimples. His haircut was very low and tapered perfectly around the sides. He had tattoos all over his arms and I could tell they circled around his neck. Izra reminded me of a male model. He looked to be only nineteen or twenty; he looked younger than Goon.

"Follow me," Goon said with his back turned towards me.

I had not seen the back of him naked until now. He was the same man I saw in the woods with the unique tattoos covering his back that leaped up into the tree. This entire time I had been thinking I was losing my mind but I wasn't!

SOUL Publications

"Goon, she's about to hit your ass again," Izra said to him, smiling at me.

"Kanya's bites and punches don't do shit to me!" Goon said then they laughed at me.

"It was nice seeing you again, Kanya! Be easy on my nigga!" Izra said, walking down the hall.

Goon stood up at the top of the spiral staircase looking at me in all of his chiseled naked glory, dick swinging between his legs. As sexy as it looked, I still wanted to rip his throat out.

"What dirty thoughts you have!" he said, smirking. I forgot the sick bastard could read my mind.

"Bring yo' ass up here, Kanya!" he said to me with bass in his voice.

I stomped up the rest of the stairs until I stood in front of him. I followed him to the end of the hall. He opened up a door and I walked into a very spacious and beautifully decorated room with stone walls and a massive fireplace. His bed was like no other! Ten people could sleep in it. It looked so cozy yet so mannish. He went into his bathroom then I heard water running. Tears fell from my eyes as I collapsed on the floor.

"This isn't normal! Shit like this doesn't exist!" I said to him.

"If heaven and hell exists so does the world we come from. Our ancestors are immortals, Kanya! It's in our blood and it's something we have to live with," Goon said to me.

SOUL Publications

"We are beasts!" I yelled at him.

"From ancient gods! We are strong, Kanya! The society we live in now cannot hurt us! Now, come and join me in the tub so I can tell you everything," he said, picking me up as if I weighed one-hundred pounds.

He walked me into the bathroom then sat me down in a tub that was built into the floor. It looked like a small pool; I saw images of this in textbooks when we studied ancient history in high school. He poured some oil into the tub and it relaxed me. It made my body tingle all over.

"This stuff is very good. Amadi makes it himself. You will meet the rest of the pack when they come back from hunting," he said to me.

"Hunting?" I asked him.

"It's how we mainly survive. We hunt for our food for fresh meat. The raw meat at the grocery store isn't fresh enough for us," he replied.

He eased himself in the tub pulling me closer to him. More tattoos started to appear on his arms, chest and legs. I jumped up, as it painfully etched through his skin like an etch-a-sketch.

"What the hell is that?" I asked him.

"I made some of them disappear when I was around you. I did not want you to see all of them. Now that you know who we are I do not have to hide them. It hurts like hell when I get a new one. If I didn't hide them you would've figured out I was the man in the woods," he laughed.

His body was beautiful. The markings made him stand out even more. And he told me everything. He told me about him being reincarnated and how his life repeats itself when he does not mate. He told me the story about my ancestors who have jackal blood. Despite his honesty, I still couldn't grasp it.

"So, that's why I have been having these strong arousal spells? I need to mate? I don't want any babies!" I spat at him. After I told him that, anger flashed in eyes and he pushed me away.

"It's not the babies you are worried about! You are afraid that they will be beasts, which they are! It is a gift not a curse! What do you want, Kanya? You want to have a baby by a human? That's what your ancestor did and it still didn't take away the genes!" he spat.

"I'm scared! Do I really have to mate?" I asked him.

"If you don't mate, you will forever be in heat. The more time passes it will only get worse. It's fate and whether you like it or not we are destined to be together," Goon said to me.

"When are we supposed to mate?" I asked, looking into his eyes.

"The next full moon is in a few months. You are in heat now but I can't get you pregnant until then," he replied.

"We are breeding?" I asked him.

SOUL Publications

"We are mating and when we do, it's for life," he said as chills ran down my spine.

"I need a drink," I said. Goon washed my body; he was very gentle and caring. He was everything I dreamt about in the past. After he helped me dry off, I climbed into his huge soft bed. He climbed in behind me, wrapping his arms around me, pulling me against him. I felt so relieved and relaxed. I wanted to be mad but his warmth and gentleness wouldn't allow me to be. I now understood why I loved him. It was destined for me to feel this way for him. He was mine and I was his.

"Where am I going to get clothes from?" I asked Goon.

"I already have clothes here for you. As soon as I found out who you were to me, I went shopping," he said. I sat up in bed then looked at him. "Let me see, I need a good laugh! What did you pick out for me? Let's see your taste," I said to him.

He chuckled then got out of the bed heading to his closet with tall double-steel doors. He walked in; when he came back out, he had outfits in his hands that made my mouth drop.

"This is so cute! How did you know my style?" I asked, looking at all of the skinny stretch jeans, fashionable leather jackets, and nice sweaters and shirts. These clothes looked better than the ones I had at home!

"I'm your soulmate. I'm supposed to know," he said arrogantly.

"You've been with a lot of women haven't you?" I asked.

"Wolves are very sexual animals. I have been with thousands of women in this life. I can't remember my other lives before I was reincarnated. When I am born again, my memory is fresh. In this life, I was born in 1850 and I have been with many women. But none of them pleased me as much as you do," he said. *"No wonder he's so skillful in the bedroom,"* I said to myself.

"Stay away from Xavier. His only concern is the scent that drips from your pussy. That scent is only made for me," Goon stated cockily.

Just a week ago, my life was normal. Yet, in a short period of time, I turned into an animal and I now had a possessive and arrogant soulmate!

"Let me guess, Xavier is a wolf, too?" I asked then he nodded his head. *"This is a bunch of bullshit!"* I thought.

"Goon, do me a favor before you get back in bed…" I said to him.

"You want a drink? Two shots of Tequila with lime and a glass of Moscato wine," he said, putting on sweatpants.

"Seriously?" I asked him.

"I can read your mind, Kanya. Once we mate, you will be able to reads mine, too," he said then smirked. "I will have Izra roll you up a blunt, too," he said, making me feel embarrassed.

I wanted my small cravings for weed to be a secret. It took Goon less than five minutes to bring everything back to me. I hurriedly downed my shots then lit my blunt up; Goon was giving me the side-eye.

"What is it, Goon?" I asked him.

"You trying to get fucked up, aren't you?" he asked me. What did he expect? My life was out of control.

"I have every right to and more!" I replied.

The weed made me throb uncontrollably and a low growl escaped Goon's throat. He smelled my scent! My nipples started to ache and a whine slipped from my throat again. The spells I had been going through were driving me crazy. I started sweating and my heart rate sped up. I climbed on top of Goon, feeling some type of erotic high. His hands gripped my hips; I went into his pants pulling out his beautiful oversized dick. I lifted my ass up, and then slid down on him. I rocked slowly then circled my hips on him; he grabbed my breasts and massaged my nipples.

He knew they ached, so he sat up and licked them with so much pressure I cried out. My nails grew long and pointy; they scratched his back. That turned him on even more; his dick swelled inside of me. A loud growl escaped his throat making the pictures on the walls fall to the floor. He thrusted into me deeply, making tears fall from my eyes. He was too big for me but the pain was beautiful. I sank my teeth into his throat; he rolled me over landing on top of me. He raised his body up then pounded into me, causing me to scream out. My wetness sprayed out of me, making him go harder and faster. He licked my lips then kissed them, as my legs wrapped around his waist. My nails shredded his sheets as I pulled on them. After I climaxed, he followed behind me.

****

The next morning, I met the whole pack personally. I saw them with Goon at the club but I did not know their names. Everyone was welcoming except for Dayo. He didn't seem too fond of me. Amadi gave me some more oils that smelled so good I could not wait to bathe in them. Kofi was very nice and I could tell he was older. Goon and Izra looked the youngest of them all. Elle was like the uncle, Amadi seemed to take care of the house and the land, and Izra was just the pain in everyone's ass!

Everyone sat down and ate breakfast; we ate slightly cooked steaks with scrambled eggs. Dayo kept looking at me from the other side of the huge dining room table.

"Is there a problem, Dayo?" Goon asked him with his temperature rising. I squeezed his arm to tell him to calm down; I could hear the growl in his voice indicating he was pissed off.

"Why the fuck is she here? Since when do you bring pussy home?" Dayo asked Goon.

"Awww shit!" Elle and Amadi said, pushing themselves away from the table. Izra grilled Dayo and Kofi sat nervously chewing his steak.

Goon leaped across the table, and by the time he knocked Dayo onto the floor, he was in wolf form. I jumped up horrified because Dayo shifted and they were biting the heck out of each other. Goon's wolf was more

94

A Beauty to His Beast: An Urban Werewolf Story   Natavia

aggressive. They rumbled into the table clawing and biting each other's necks. The table broke in half and all of our food went crashing to the floor.

"Cut it out!" Kofi yelled but they were not listening.

"Fuck his ass up, Goon!" Izra egged him on while eating his food from the plate on his lap. The scene was almost comical if there were not two large animals shredding each other apart. Goon sank his teeth into Dayo's neck then slung him into the wall like a stuffed animal.

"GOON, STOP IT! YOU ARE GOING TO KILL HIM!" I screamed.

Goon stopped then backed away from Dayo. Goon shifted back standing before us naked with bite marks and bloody deep gashes on his body. I cringed at his open wounds revealing flesh. After a few seconds, his wounds started to close up. The rest of the wolves looked at him then gasped at how quickly he was healing. Dayo shifted back with bite marks and deep open claw marks everywhere on his body. My hand covered my mouth because Dayo's face was unrecognizable. The other wolves tended to him as they all helped him up. All except for Izra and Goon, of course.

"Is he okay?" I asked Kofi concerned.

"Yes, he will be fine and looking brand new in a few days. His wounds will close up eventually," Kofi said as they carried him out of the dining room.

"That damn Goon knocked over the fucking orange juice!" Izra complained as he stared at his broken glass on the floor.

I went into Goon's room; he was sitting by the window wearing sweatpants. "I don't want to hear it, Kanya!" he said, reading my mind.

"You were so aggressive! You could've killed him!" I said to him.

"I don't give a fuck about him! Pack brother or not, he needs to have some respect!" Goon said sternly.

"You need to control your temper!" I said to him.

He chuckled. "The pot calling the kettle black I see. Weren't you trying to chase me down last night? As I recall you even bit me! And you punched me in the eye!" he said making me laugh.

"That doesn't count! You said it didn't hurt!" I said, laughing.

"Naw, it was cute though. Feisty little jackal," he chuckled.

"Is my beast really that small?" I asked then he fell over laughing showing his white perfect teeth. When Goon wasn't serious his boyish looks were very noticeable.

"You aren't as big as a wolf but you are still my little beast! A pretty one at that!" he said, making me blush.

"Are you sweet talking me?" I asked him.

"Is it working?" he replied.

I hugged him inhaling his scent and it was different. It wasn't a cologne scent but like a sweet but masculine type of musk.

"What are you wearing?" I asked him.

"Since you've shifted, you can smell my scent. The more we are around each other, the stronger our connection will become," he said, kissing my neck.

"You didn't tell me that at first. A female wolf can smell you?" I asked him, getting agitated. I was past jealous! I was furious! Goon's scent was alluring. It screamed Alpha male!

"I'm only concerned about Kanya. However, if you want to fight me, I would rather for you to shift first. I could use a little exercise," he said, rubbing on my butt.

I smacked his hands away; he playfully pushed me on the bed then started kissing my neck. Seconds later, Goon had me pinned down with his dick buried deep inside of me. After Goon and I showered, we got dressed to head out for the day. Adika wanted me to hang out with her; it had been awhile since the two of us did something together. After Goon and I spent our day together, he took me over to Adika's house. When he pulled up in front of the building, he looked at me smirking—he knew I didn't want to leave him.

"What's the matter with you? You are going to miss me, aren't you?" Goon asked, caressing my face.

"No, I'm not!" I said pouting.

"Get your ass out of my truck then!" he said smiling.

SOUL Publications

I rolled my eyes at him then pinched his arm with my long sharp nails. It still hurts when they break through my skin but my body was adjusting to it. He slightly growled and then his eyes turned blue.

"That shit got me hard!" he said.

I hurriedly exited the truck before I got in one of those spells where I couldn't control my hormones.

"Let me know when you want me to pick you up," he said in my head but he was still smiling at me. That was creepy! I kept telling Goon to stop popping up in my head like that.

"Please, Goon. That shit scares me. And don't be in my head while Adika and I are having girl talk," I said then he smirked.

I waved him off after he pulled off. I walked into Adika's apartment building. When I got to her door, she had the radio blasting playing one of Lil Boosie's songs. I knocked on her door as hard as I could. She opened it up a few moments later blowing weed in my face.

"Are you partying without me?" I asked, walking into her apartment. She giggled then sipped her glass of wine.

"Yes! I'm on vacation from both jobs for a week. I'm about to get loose," she said, popping her butt out.

I missed hanging out with Adika, the partying, the clubbing and the shopping. I missed it all! Nevertheless, when she had free time, which was one night out of the month, she always spent it with me. Our friendship was unbreakable! She poured me a glass of wine then sat down across from me.

"So, tell me. What is going on with you and Goon? Girl, you got the stank walk now! He must've given you a lot of pipe!" she laughed.

If only she knew how much pipe I have been taking! I thought to myself.

"He is wonderful, Adika. He is rough around the edges and can be a smart-ass but he is such a wonderful man! He runs my bath water, caters to my body and me. He spoils me! Our connection is spiritual," I told her.

"That's wonderful! I'm proud for you," she said smiling.

"Sasha thinks I'm moving too fast," I said to her.

"Honey, let me tell you something. Feelings don't come with a time frame. Some people fall in love at first sight. Do not listen to Sasha. She is a cool person but I wouldn't be surprised if she didn't want him for herself," Adika said.

"Why would you say that?" I asked her.

"What other reason would she have to not like the fact that you are finally happy? I don't care if you met him five damn minutes ago! Seeing you glowing means a lot to me. I was there when you and Jason broke up. Honey, live it up! Hell, does Goon have a brother?" Adika asked me.

"He has a five of them!" I said to her.

SOUL Publications

"Get the hell out of here! Are they fine? Damn, you almost gave me an orgasm!" She fanned herself.

"Yes, they are very attractive but other than Goon, Izra is breathtakingly handsome! He just has a problem with his choice of words," I said.

"Hell, that can be fixed!" Adika said.

A part of me wanted to tell Adika what I am and what Goon is but I don't think I can bring myself to do it. I'm still trying to accept the truth myself.

"I'm not dressed for the club, Adika!" I said to her as I rode in the passenger seat of her car.

"Yes, you are! You have on pumps and skinny jeans with a blazer," she said to me. When we arrived at the hookah lounge in Baltimore City, the line was extremely long.

"Why didn't you tell me you were going out to a club?" Goon's voice spat angrily in my head. I dropped my purse because he was too loud and it scared the hell out of me.

"Are you okay?" Adika asked, picking up my purse.

"Yes, I'm fine," I told her.

"I thought you wasn't going to do that!" I said in my head.

"I wasn't until I pulled up and saw you getting out of her car!" Goon spat back.

I looked around then his scent tingled my nose. I followed it and there he was in the parking lot looking handsomely rugged. He wore a fitted black sweater-like hoodie that hugged his muscular frame. His jeans fit him perfectly and he wore a pair of black Polo boots. Izra was in the parking lot with him smoking a blunt. Adika cleared her throat; she wanted me to introduce her to Izra.

"Izra, this is my best friend, Adika. Adika, this is Goon's brother, Izra," I said, putting my arm through Goon's arm. Izra lustfully eyed Adika up and down then smirked.

"What's up, shorty?" he said, pulling her to his side. They started chatting but we ignored them.

"Why are you and Izra different from the other pack brothers? You two fit in, but everyone else seems stuck in time," I said to Goon.

"That's because Izra and I get out more and interact with society. The others come out sometimes but they spend most of their time traveling," Goon said.

Once we ended up in the lounge, we got a small section to ourselves. The waitress went to get our bottles while Adika and I blew smoke out of our mouths from the hookah.

"Did you know I was coming here?" I asked Goon.

"Nope, I didn't invade your privacy. Izra and I always come here when there isn't shit else for us to do," Goon answered. Adika and Izra were smiling and laughing all in each other's faces.

"Izra must be pleased with her scent," Goon said laughing.

A few drinks and an hour later, I was buzzed. Beyoncé's "711" song came on; I stood up pulling Adika to the dancefloor. I was having more fun than I had ever had. I just had a jolt of happiness within me all of a sudden. I felt so alive! I felt free! The feeling was amazing! I told Adika I would be right back as I headed towards the bathroom. Surprisingly, it was clean and empty. I hated using the club bathrooms. After I took care of my business, I wiped myself then flushed the toilet. While I was washing my hands, I heard someone come in.

"What are you doing in here?" I said aloud, never looking up.
"Your nose is getting better, I see!" Goon said, locking the bathroom door. I dried my hands off. "What do you want?" I asked him, blushing.

He was by the door then in a split second, he was kissing my lips; he was fast! He undid my pants then stuck his hand in my panties massaging my swollen bud.

"Do me a favor," he said, biting my earlobe as his finger slid into me causing me to moan aloud.

"What?" I asked, panting.

"Never pop your ass out like that again! I'd rather for my shows to be given in private!" he said, sliding his finger further into me making my knees buckle. I fell into him as he held me up from under my ass making me orgasm.

Goon

One month later...

*D*ayo healed up perfectly but he hasn't been coming around me as much. Xavier and his pack have been quiet. I'd been around his club a few times but was not able to track him. What he did to Izra and then coming on our land was still unacceptable. I had a feeling he would resurface again.

I walked down the opposite side of the hall and knocked on Kofi's door. He had been quiet lately and very seldom came out of his room. All I heard throughout the hall was loud orchestra music playing. Kofi wasn't too pleased with this century. The music, the fashion and the technology, he hated it all. I knocked on his door; Kofi opened it up wearing a robe puffing on a cigar. When he found me in the woods back in 1860, he looked to be around thirty. Now he looks only forty. Werewolves age slowly!

I walked into his room then sat down at his desk; he sat down behind it.

"What's troubling you?" Kofi asked.

"I'm leaving the pack," I said to him.

"I don't understand. Why would you do such a thing? This pack has been together for years! I saw you grow from a pup to a mighty wolf," he said, his feelings hurt.

SOUL Publications

"I'm different from everybody else. I don't fit in. You all are wolves from ancestry. I'm a wolf from an Ancient Egyptian god with a witch as my mother," I said then he smiled.

"Keora told you everything, huh?" Kofi asked me. I'm assuming that was Mrs. Carroll's real name.

"You knew what I was since I was a young pup, didn't you?" I asked him. Kofi is the one who sent me to Mrs. Carroll and now I knew why.

"I was sent from the immortal world to protect you. I couldn't bring myself to tell you because I didn't want to upset you. So, I wanted you to hear it from someone else. My job is done now. The next full moon the portal to the immortal world will open up for me and I will return. For years, I have been away from my mate to serve your father. Now it is time for me to go back home. My job was to guide you and make sure you found your mate. You don't remember because you have been reincarnated more times than I can count; I have been your protector in all of your lives. I really miss home!" Kofi said to me.

"Damn it!" I said standing up. I paced back and forth. "You knew Kanya was going to come into the woods that night while I was hunting. That's why you sent me there?" I asked him.

"Your parents knew and they informed me. She is a re-markable woman by the way. Very feisty. She reminds me of my mate, who is a jackal, too. She is Kanya's greatest grandmother," he said to me.

"This shit is too much," I said.

"You know who you are now, Goon. You know who your mate is. However, you cannot leave your pack. That's brotherhood. Your father made them like warriors to protect you. Especially Izra," he said to me.

"How do I tell them what I really am?" I asked him.

"You don't have to tell them. Show them who you really are and they will follow," Kofi replied.

After Kofi and I talked, I headed back to my room. I promised Kanya I would pick her up in time from work. She stopped being hardheaded and never went back to work at the club. After I showered and got dressed, I headed out of the door. When I pulled up to the nursing home, Kanya was sitting on the bench with tears falling from her face. I hurriedly got out of my truck.

"What's the matter with you?" I asked her.

"Mrs. Carroll died!" she sobbed then I laughed.

"What did she die from?" I asked her.

I never told Kanya who Mrs. Carroll was and that she wasn't really any kin to me.

"Damn it, Goon, she is your grandmother, isn't she? No, wait a minute! She really isn't, is she? You are older than her! What's going on?" Kanya asked me.

"Carroll is an old witch. She was just a friend of the family. It was her time to go," I told her then her face dropped.

SOUL Publications

"What the fuck! What's next Goon? Are there vampires, too? This is just too damn much! I even did CPR on her because she choked off a chicken bone! I lost my damn job because they said I could've saved her!" Kanya spat.

"There are vampires, too, but they don't look the way we think they do. They are not pale-like with red eyes. They are ugly-looking oversized bats and they live in caves," I said to her.

"I'm scared of this. I'm afraid of it all!" she said, wiping her eyes.

"I'm your protector, Kanya. You don't have to be afraid," I said to her.

Kanya got up then walked towards my truck. A small Jeep pulled up next to me as I stepped off the sidewalk. The driver looked to be a college student with a University of Maryland sweatshirt on. Her hair was pulled back into a ponytail and her skin was the color of cinnamon.

"Excuse me, can you tell where the next gas station is?" she asked me.

"Cut the shit, Keora!" I laughed then she smiled.

"So, you finally know my name?" Keora asked me.

"Yeah, I like the new you better," I said, dropping a diamond necklace on her passenger seat.

She looked at it then smiled. "This is beautiful! You beasts are sitting on a gold mine," she stated.

"Okay, let me get going. I have class in a few hours. I want to know how Kanya would feel if she knew you wanted her to get fired," she said to me then laughed.

"You are a real bitch, you know that?" I chuckled. She gave me the finger then sped off.

When I turned around, Kanya was grilling me with her arms crossed. I hope she did not hear our conversation. Then again, I would have known if she did because her mind is linked to mine.

"Were you flirting with that woman?" Kanya asked me.

"No, that was just someone who needed directions!" I said to her. Her eyes cut into me then she grilled me again.

"I can't read your mind yet but I know when you are lying! Your ass is lying, Goon! Now, who was that woman and what did she want?" Kanya asked me.

I smirked. "Jealous aren't you?"

I know she couldn't help it if she wanted to. She was supposed to feel all the emotions she had for me; our bond was made this way.

"You are lying to me!" she said, stomping off back towards my truck.

When I got inside, she was ignoring me. When Kanya throws her fits, it was always hysterical. I knew it came from me spoiling her but I'm supposed to. She did not need to work! She wasn't supposed to work! The Alpha male always takes care of his mate!

"I didn't know witches died! Aren't they immortal also?" she asked me.

"She was very old," I said.

"We mate next month. Aren't we supposed to be baby shopping or something? Oh god, I cannot believe we are going to be having pups!" she said.

"Don't worry about that. It lasts for only two months," I said to her.

"WHAT!" she screamed.

"Your pregnancy will only last for two months. Our pups will be immortal, Kanya," I told her.

"I was finally getting excited about carrying a child! Now, you are telling me I will not be able to experience the feeling from it. Two damn months? That means my stomach is going to show within a week! People are going to be suspicious about that! We still have to live in society with people! What will the doctors think?" Kanya ranted.

"We will have to relocate to a different area if we don't figure it out by then and we don't need a doctor! This is not a human pregnancy, Kanya!" I said to her.

When I pulled up to the house, Kanya got out of the truck slamming my door. She walked into the house then headed straight to my bedroom. The heavy door slammed, echoing throughout the house.

Kofi walked down the stairs. "Don't worry, Goon. My mate almost killed me once. She locked jaw on my neck.

Jackals are very beautiful but their attitudes are not. Only love can get you through it." Kofi laughed then patted me on the shoulder.

Kanya bit me two nights ago when she shifted on me. I was still in human form when she attacked me. It was hard for me to keep my beast in because if I hadn't, I would've attacked her and possibly killed her.

When I walked into my room, Kanya's clothes were in shreds on the floor. I heard a growl coming from the corner. Kanya shifted and was now in her beast form. She paced back and forth with her bushy tale sticking straight up. Her gold claws scratched the floor with every step she took. Her ears were pointed back and she had a scowl on her face. I shifted into my form so she wouldn't attack me. Kanya was still afraid of my beast. I walked over to her and then licked her face. She rubbed her head against mine and then licked me. She was no longer angry.

"Aye, Goon, are you trying to go strip club with me tonight?" Izra asked, barging into my room.

He looked at Kanya and I then smiled. "I need to take a picture of this! A wolf and a Pomeranian!" Izra laughed because Kanya's wolf form was smaller than ours. She leaped on the wall then jumped on Izra, knocking him into my bathroom and breaking the door.

"Damn it, Goon! Get this damn dog off me! Her fucking bites hurt like shit! ARRRGGHHHHHHH!" Izra yelled.

I laughed as Kanya dragged Izra across the floor by his pants leg. Amadi, Dayo and Elle stood in my doorway with their mouths open. They had never seen her shift before; I hadn't told them yet what she was. I had not even told them what I was. Although Kofi stated that I could not leave my pack, I was still thinking about doing so. I shifted back to human form.

"Cut that shit out, Kanya!" I yelled out. She growled then let Izra go.

"I'm calling the animal shelter on her ass!" Izra said out of breath.

Kanya looked at Dayo then leaped on him, biting his shoulder. He rolled down the stairs with Kanya on top of him. Kanya was a new shifter; she had yet to control herself. I tried to pull Kanya off Dayo but he shifted to wolf form. Dayo threw Kanya across the room. I wanted her to fight him back but if he hurt her, I was going to kill him. She got up then crawled up the wall, leaping on him and clamping down on his neck then rolled him over. I noticed that she moved quicker than all of us; she moved like a hunter. Dayo whimpered as we watched Kanya roll him over.

"Hunting is in a jackal's nature! She is very fast!" Kofi said to me.
"That's enough, Kanya!" I said to her then she stopped. She shifted back to human form and was now standing in front of my pack brothers naked!

"Oh my!" Amadi said. I hurriedly picked her up then ran upstairs with her. Once we got back to my room, I slammed my door.

"What the fuck did you do that for? You are not supposed to shift back in front of them! They saw all of you!" I yelled at her.

SOUL Publications

"I can't help when I shift! I didn't want to shift in the first place! I was mad when I came here, then all of sudden I was a beast!" she spat.

"Why did you attack Dayo like that?" I asked her.

"Dayo wants my fucking man, that's why! I saw him stare lustfully at you when you shifted back to human form! He couldn't keep his eyes off your dick! He even got an erection from it!" she said walking into the bathroom.

"I didn't see that! Wolves aren't into the same sex. Although, we are very sexual and have sex a lot, we never get intimate with the same sex. Humans do it but we aren't supposed to be that way," I said to her.

"I'm sure you didn't see it. You all are used to seeing each other like that. However, I saw it in his eyes, Goon. That's why he acts like he hates you so much. Probably so you will not read his mind and figure it out. I'm a woman and I know what the hell it is. He looked at you the same way I did when I first saw you. That's why he is mad because I'm here. Wait till he finds out you are getting me pregnant," she stated.

"You have gone mad, Kanya! Werewolves are not gay!" I said to her.

"What the hell was he staring at your dick for then, Goon? Explain that shit to me! Explain how not everyone else gave a damn about your dick swinging! The only one who was lustfully staring was Dayo! He is jealous of me!" Kanya screamed.

"I don't believe it, Kanya! We've been in the same pack for one-hundred and fifty years and not once have I seen him look at me that way or read his mind about another man!" I said to her.

"Whatever, Goon! See what you want but I'll tell you this, if he does it again I'm scratching his eyes out!" she said, turning on the shower. When she came back out of the bathroom, she started to get dressed.

"Where are you going?" I asked her, sitting up on the bed.

"Sasha and I are going out. She just called and asked me if I wanted to go out for some drinks," Kanya stated.

"I don't like that sneaky bitch!" I told Kanya.

"Don't call her that! She isn't that bad!" Kanya laughed.

"How long are you going to be out for?" I was trying my hardest to deal with Kanya going out now. I didn't care if she went out with Adika but Sasha was up to something.

"Not long, I promise!" she said, trying to kiss my lips but I pushed her out of the way then stood up towering over her.

"This shit is getting complicated!" I told Kanya.

"What is complicated? I have a life outside of this, Goon. I'm still young and I still want to do things," she said.

"I know and I'm still trying to understand all of this! This is new for me, too! Where is Adika?" I asked her.

"She and Izra are going out on their first date. I can't wait till she tells me about it," Kanya beamed.

"Don't you want to hang out with some other friends?" I asked Kanya.

"I don't have any other friends! Can I take your truck?" she asked me.

"Go ahead! I'd better not smell that bitch's scent in my truck when I get in there tomorrow neither! I mean it, Kanya! I would shift; go to her house and scare the hell out of her!" I spat.

Kanya rolled her eyes at me then switched out of my room in her tight pants. I wanted to yank her up and demand she change her clothes but I couldn't. I still wanted Kanya to do the things that she is used to and although she is my soulmate I didn't want to force it on her. I smelled food cooking then walked downstairs into the kitchen. Amadi, Elle, and Kofi were having drinks and Izra was smoking a blunt talking on his cell-phone. I took the blunt from him then smoked it. I grabbed the bottle of Henny off the island then took it to the head.

"What's the matter, Goon?" Elle asked me.

"Woman problems I bet," Amadi said then chuckled.

"He will be alright! He has to get used to it because his problems from here on out are going to get worse! He and Kanya have possessive issues!" Kofi said, puffing his cigar.

"What is Kanya? She looks like a wolf but she doesn't smell like one!" Amadi said.

"She's a Jackal," I said to him.

"Jackals appear every thousands of years or so. And when they do it's to mate with an Alpha male I heard," Amadi said.

"So, Goon is the Alpha male?" Elle asked Kofi.

"Look, it doesn't matter who is what. After she and I mate for eternity, I'm leaving the pack," I said downing the rest of the liquor.

Izra hung up the phone. "Nigga, you didn't run that shit by me! You can't leave the pack! This is tradition and it has been passed down from our ancestors! It is a brotherhood, although Dayo's fruity ass can leave! Matter of fact, Dayo needs to be a poodle!" Izra said. Dayo walked into the kitchen with a scowl on his face.

"You got something you want to say to me?" Dayo asked Izra.

"This gay-ass nigga!" Izra said aloud.

"This behavior between y'all has been unacceptable!" Elle's voice boomed. Amadi started cutting up a slab of raw meat. I took a piece of it then tossed it up, catching it with my teeth then swallowed it.

"Amadi, what's up with you looking at my woman's pussy? You know I saw you, right?" I asked him then everyone laughed.

"Goon, you my nigga and all, but everyone was looking at that fat twat! Everyone except for Dayo's bitch-ass!"

Izra stated. Dayo tried to charge into Izra but Elle pushed him back.

"Dayo, I would fuck you up! I'm telling you, bro! I would so don't try that shit again!" Izra said to Dayo.

"Wolves are not gay! Stop saying that shit!" Elle yelled at Izra.

Izra waved Elle off then walked out of the kitchen pissed off. Dayo looked at me then I grilled him. When I read his mind, all he was doing was cursing Izra. Dayo snatched away from Elle then walked out of the kitchen.

"I'm done babysitting!" Kofi spat, walking away.

I knew what he really meant. He was tired of looking out for us and I could see that he missed his mate. Kofi was slipping into depression. He had never isolated himself away from everyone like this before.

"Where are you at now?" I asked Kanya inside my head.

"Damn it, Goon! Use your cell-phone! You almost made me swerve this big ass truck off the road!" she panicked. Her smooth soft voice hardened my dick.

"Are you wet right now? Come back real quick!" I said to her.

"NO!" she laughed.

"Okay cool! Holla at me when you get situated! I'm just going to chill with Amadi and Elle," I said to her.

"Be on good behavior," Kanya told me.

"What's it like having to be tied down to one woman for the rest of your life?" Amadi asked me as he poured himself a glass of Henny.

"It's hard sometimes; she didn't even know what she was until I brought it out of her. She fights what she is and at times she looks at me in horror when I shift," I told him.

"She is a good woman though. Her conversations are interesting," Amadi said.

"So, you two are in love?" Elle asked me.

"I don't know what love really is, Elle. I have never been in it before but what I'm experiencing might be it," I chuckled then they laughed. I ended up getting drunk and telling Amadi and Elle everything else I'd learned about Kanya and me.

Izra was gone on his date with Adika, everyone else went to their rooms. Dayo usually went to sleep early because he woke up early to hunt. I stood by his door then looked around. I disappeared then reappeared in his room. He was snoring loudly; I crawled up the wall in a dark corner of his room.

He was dreaming about me when I entered his mind. His thoughts were sick! His hand slid down on his dick, touching himself. Thoughts of me bending him over and taking him in the same way I took Kanya was making him aroused. My growl echoed throughout his room. When he woke up, I disappeared and was on the other side of the door in the hallway. I hurriedly went into my room and threw up everything that was in my stomach. *"My pack brother was in lust over me! Kanya was right!"* I thought to myself.

Xavier

I had been gone for a month because my wounds were healing slowly… *Very* slowly. Aki and I were back to normal and now I was ready to strike back! Goon's pack brother had done a lot of damage to us. Aki almost died twice because he lost a lot of blood. Usually we healed in a few days but not this time. I was at my father's house, pacing back and forth trying to come up with a plan to get rid of Goon and his pack. Not to mention, take Kanya away from him. She didn't belong with him. She belonged to me and I did not care what anyone else said!

"You are just getting back and you are already thinking?" my father asked me.

"Those wolves are dangerous!" I shouted at him.

"Those wolves are built to protect the son of Ammon! That's why you healed slowly. Ammon is not pleased that you are trying to mess with his son," my father said to me.

"Are you scared of him? Isn't he just a spirit trapped in some kind of immortal ancient Egypt world?" I laughed. My father shook his head.

"You are going to ruin this pack. It is not supposed to be like this. If you and Goon fight and he wins, he will take over your pack. You will have to bow down to him. Just walk away, Xavier, and let it go. You should not have gone to his home. You never step foot on another pack's homeland! Have I not taught you anything. I taught you how to become an Alpha male and you are upsetting me and the immortal gods!" my father said.

My phone rang and it was Aki. "Talk to me!" I said walking out of the room as my father ranted on.

"Sasha is meeting us and she has Kanya with her," Aki said. A smile spread across my face as I thought of myself entering Kanya's body with her welcoming alluring scent.

"Okay, great," I said hanging up.

"She is not yours to mate with, Xavier! Goon's father stamped her just for him and only him! I wouldn't get too close to her if I was you," he said to me.

"I don't want to mate with her! She can give him as many pups as she wants! I just have to have her once!" I told him before I walked out of his house.

Amilia called my phone. "WHAT!" I spat when I answered.

"What time are you coming home? I'm waiting!" she purred.

"Continue to wait because I have things to do, Amilia!" I said, hanging up on her.

I arrived at the address Aki gave me and it was a lounge and bar on the outskirts of the city. This area was perfect! I got out of my car and Aki was waiting for me by the door. He still had a long scratch on his neck that I think will never go away; he was scarred for life. When we walked into the lounge, Sasha and Kanya were sitting down at the table laughing and chatting. Kanya's sexiness had gone up a notch; her breasts were rounder and fuller and she had a glow to her. It was that son-of-a-bitch fucking her, making her look that way.

"There you are!" Sasha got up then hugged Aki. Kanya looked uncomfortable when she saw me. I smirked because I know her mate told her to stay away from me.

"Kanya, this is Aki! Well, I know you met him before since he and Xavier are friends but he and I have been dating," Sasha told Kanya. Kanya spit her drink out then wiped her mouth.

"You set this up? A double date?" Kanya yelled at Sasha.

"What is the matter with you? I can't help that Xavier came with him," Sasha lied.

"I'm out of here! You can have fun by your damn self. You are lucky I have on my cute pumps or else I would beat your ass!" Kanya threatened Sasha.

Sasha covered her mouth shocked by Kanya's threat. Kanya got up then bumped into Sasha, sending her flying into a table across the lounge. Aki looked at me with a confused look on his face. That wasn't just human strength! It would take more than one person to send someone across the room like that. I followed Kanya out of the lounge. Her hips swayed side to side and her ass bounced with each stride she took in her high-heels. The men were looking at her lustfully; she held a lot of sex appeal and it was intoxicating. I could not smell her scent because she wasn't aroused and because I'm not her soulmate. Only Goon could smell Kanya's scent at any time. She tried getting into a truck but I slightly pulled her away from the door.

Her eyes flashed gold then a growl slipped from her throat. Her canines grew out and her nails grew long and pointy turning gold. They sparkled underneath the parking lot lights.

"Don't touch me! I know what you want from me and you are not getting it! Now move out of my way!" she said, pushing me aside. I looked around to make sure no one saw me. I picked her up then ran to the woods as she clawed and bit me.

"Stop fighting me!" I told her as I slammed her against a tree.

She howled out in pain and that is when I ripped her pants and panties off. She clawed at my face opening my skin up; she bit my neck. Kanya was not as strong as me and if she was a new shifter, she would not shift as quickly. I threw her down on the ground and her head slammed against a rock. I was not going to rape her; I just wanted to taste her! I forced her legs opened then stuck my tongue inside of her. She tried to fight me off but she was weak from hitting her head.

"Please stop!" Kanya screamed.

She was getting aroused, even when she didn't want to. Her scent filled my nostrils then I gently bit down on her bud sending my saliva into her body. My scent was going to be inside of her, letting Goon know I was with her. I forced her legs up then growled licking between her swollen lips. I could feel her pussy clench as she was about to release. She was going to come inside my mouth. She tasted so sweet! My hard-on pressed against my pants as semen dripped from the tip of my shaft. I sucked her clit harder, sinking my teeth into her. She let out a piercing scream as she clawed at me scratching my face and neck. Her legs shook as she came again. She stopped fighting me then moaned when I slid my finger into her. Her wetness splashed onto the mushy ground in the woods. She was in heat and could not resist the pleasure.

Kanya

I tried to shift to fight him off but I couldn't! Goon said it would take time for me to shift when I wanted to. I laid in the grass in the woods as Xavier brought me multiple orgasms. My body burned and my nipples ached to be sucked. All of sudden, Xavier was lifted off me then tossed into the air. I hurriedly sat up then hid behind a tree. Goon's wolf leaped into the air then caught Xavier by the throat slamming him into a tree. Xavier shifted then bit Goon on his shoulder. They started rolling around biting and clawing each other. Their loud growls echoed throughout the woods. Goon sank his teeth into Xavier's neck then slung him into a tree again; the tree fell down as the two big wolves attacked each other. Xavier's wolf was almost as big as Goon's. I heard more growls then I turned around. Two more wolves appeared out of the bushes then jumped on Goon. Xavier set him up! All of this was a setup to ambush Goon.

My body fell over as I screamed out in pain; my clothes shredded away from my body. A growl escaped my throat and my nails felt like knives piercing through my skin. I turned into my beast. While Goon tried fighting the three wolves off him, I charged into the brawl, biting and clawing at the other wolves. One of them slammed me into a tree; Goon shook the other two off him then charged into the one that slammed me. Goon's eyes started glowing and the tribal markings on him glowed throughout his fur. His teeth sank into the wolf's neck so deeply he cracked its spine, killing him instantly. Blood dripped from Goon's mouth as he growled at the other two who were circling him.

Three wolves came leaping from out of the trees. There were more of them! We were outnumbered! Goon stood his ground as he stood in front of me; he was going to die from protecting me. I heard howling then bushes started shaking and leaves fell from the trees. Three wolves appeared from out of the bushes with the same tribal markings in their fur like Goon's. Those had to be Kofi, Amadi, and Elle.

"Run to the house, Kanya, and don't look back! Go now!" Goon's deep voice boomed inside my head. I could not leave him. His blue eyes bore into mine and I could tell that he was angry with me. I should've listened to him! Sasha put me in this position!

Goon's pack charged into the other wolves and it was horrific! The smell of blood filled my nostrils as Goon ripped some wolves apart. I was screaming in my head because Goon appeared to be the beast that I first saw him as in the beginning, he was malicious. Xavier took off running leaving his pack behind to get brutally attacked. Goon's pack was bigger and stronger! Goon ran after Xavier and then another wolf leaped out of the tree that I did not know was there! I could tell by their face structure that it was a female. She sneakily trotted behind Goon and I followed her. I leaped up in a tree then jumped tree from tree until I had her in my view. I leaped onto her back then we rolled down a ditch into a pond. She got up then shook herself off. Her wolf was beautiful; she was all white with green eyes. She was around my size in height and length. She growled at me then I charged into her. She slashed my face and I slashed hers. We rolled around in the dirty water, biting and clawing each other. I went for her neck then slammed her into the water; she kicked me off with her hind legs, sending me into a tree.

I charged into her again, digging my nails into her face; she whimpered in pain. I clamped down onto her neck—the taste of blood made my beast more aggressive! She was trying to kick me off but I bit her face. She was bloody and she was getting weak. I stepped away from her then took off running. I did not have it in me to kill!

When I got to the mansion, I burst through the window. I know Amadi was going to shit a brick because he always has to repair the windows and doors. I ran up the stairs then burst through Goon's bedroom door. I howled out in pain as my body shifted back. I was naked and bloody with deep scratches in my skin and bite marks. I collapsed onto the floor as my human body felt the pain from being attacked by a large animal. *I'm going to die! I felt my life slipping away,"* I thought. Dayo stood in the doorway watching me bleed out onto the floor.

"Help me!" I said to him. He walked out of the room and into his, slamming his door.

Goon barged into his room shifting back to his human form. Dayo must have connected to his mind to tell him I was hurt.

"It hurts!" I said as he held me.

"What I'm about to do is going to hurt even more but it's the only way you will heal. I don't have time to give you my blood," he said cradling me. His teeth extended and he twisted my head to the side then clamped down on my neck. It was so much pressure my teeth sharpened as I howled out in pain. My nails scratched at his arm as he crushed my wind pipe. I coughed up blood then I stopped breathing. I closed my eyes then drifted off...

I woke up with a headache. I hurriedly sat up and looked around. I was in a different room but I could tell I was still at the mansion. Kofi was sitting in the chair next to my bed. He rushed to me with a glass of water and I guzzled it down until I started choking.

"Where is Goon?" I asked Kofi then he let out a deep breath.

"Goon is upstairs. He refuses to come into this room. He has been watching you from the doorway. Xavier's scent is still on you," Kofi said. I felt my neck and the rest of my body. My wounds were gone! The last thing I remembered was Goon sinking his sharp teeth into my neck.

"He healed you, Kanya. I know it was a very painful feeling but he had to act quickly because you were going to bleed out and die," Kofi said to me.

"I thought shifters don't die," I said to him.

"Oh, yes they do. They can live for decades but if you bleed out before the healing process you can die," he said, helping me sit up. Goon came down the small staircase that led to my room. Kofi excused himself; Goon stood in the doorway with anger-filled eyes.

"I'm sorry," I said to him then he chuckled.

"For what? Are you sorry that you got pleasure from him or are you sorry that you had to find out that Sasha isn't your friend? You are very hardheaded! If I hadn't entered your mind when I did, you would have fucked him! I felt your desire for him when he pleasured you! I heard your moans! I saw the vision of you letting him stick his fingers inside of you!" Goon said with his voice raising.

Tears fell from my eyes. "I couldn't control it!" I said to him.

"I know and that's why I don't think this mating shit is going to work! If another wolf can have you after I have marked you then you aren't for me. You have this room smelling just like him. His scent is in my damn house, reminding me that he was intimate with you," Goon said, punching a hole in the wall. I could see that he wanted to shift because his eyes changed blue every time he raised his voice.

I got out of bed on wobbly legs; I wanted him to hold me while I breathed in his scent. I wanted everything to go away! I wanted a normal life! I wanted the closeness he and I always shared. I stood up on my tiptoes wrapping my arms around his neck. I cried into his chest and he let me, but after a few seconds he pushed me off him, sending me sliding across the floor on my ass and into my bed.

"You fucking stink!" he yelled at me then walked up the stairs.

I heard a door slam and pictures fall on the floor shattering. Kofi ran downstairs with Elle and Amadi. They helped me up off the floor.

"Let him cool off; he has been in a funk for days. You have been asleep for three days," Elle said to me. I cried.

A week had passed and I was still at the mansion. Kofi and the rest of the pack moved items out of my apartment into the basement. They set it up just like my studio apartment. Kofi said I could not go back home because that territory did not belong to neither pack; Xavier would be able to get to me. Adika had been calling me but I have not been answering. Goon not dealing with me was making me sick! He walks past me like he doesn't see me; he ignores me and hasn't been popping up in my head. He stays out all night and doesn't come home till the morning. I know because I watch him out of the window from the time he leaves and I stay in the window until he gets back. He even saw me watching him and did not say not one word to me! I asked Kofi what happened the night the wolves got into the brawl. He stated that Xavier ran off and Goon never caught him because he had to get to me. He also said that two wolves died as well. I am glad it wasn't any one from this pack!

Izra walked into the living room with a tray of food. They all catered to me except for Goon and Dayo. Everyone else spoiled me!

"I'm not hungry," I said to Izra.

"You better eat this, Kanya. It took me two hours to hunt this bear," he said to me.

"Maryland doesn't have bears!" I said laughing.

"I went up in the mountains, hours away. I was in Virginia," he said, giving me the raw cut-up meat with steamed broccoli.

SOUL Publications

I ate my food as Izra watched me. "What do you want?" I asked him.

"You and Adika talk about sex, right?" Izra asked me.

"Of course, idiot, why wouldn't we?" I asked.

"How many men has she been with? Be honest with me!" Izra said then my mouth dropped open.

"I will not tell you that!" I said to him.

"Well, I won't help you get your man back! You do know he's mad at you right? I mean never-talk-to-you-again type of mad! Do you know he saw through your eyes when Xavier was eating your hotbox? That right there would make a beast go crazy!" Izra said, eating off my plate.

"Just rub it in!" I said, pinching him.

"How many men has she been with?" Izra asked me again.

"You really like her don't you?" I asked him then he smirked.

"She aight!" Izra replied but I knew it was more than what he was letting on. Goon came into the house with a scowl on his face. I sat my tray down then walked over to him. He looked down at me then leaned against the wall crossing his arms.

"What's going on?" he asked me.

"I miss you! Can you just talk to me, please?" I asked him.

"Yeah, we can later," he said, walking away from me. I grabbed his arm then he looked at me as if I was garbage.

"Are you sleeping with another woman?" I asked Goon.

"I'm not dealing with this!" he said, walking upstairs and away from me. A growl slipped from my throat then I leaped on him.

"Talk to me!" I screamed, shredding his hoodie sweatshirt. Izra ran up the stairs to pull me off Goon.

"Just talk to her, bro! You cannot let her carry on like this! It is almost pitiful! She's been moping around here for a whole week!" Izra said to him.

Goon's eyes softened up then he let out a deep breath. "When she gets rid of his scent, I will! A whole week has passed and it still burns my nose!" Goon said, walking up the stairs and taking off his hoodie. His back muscles flexed and his tribal markings had never looked so strong and mannish. The spiritual bond that we had was too powerful! Goon not talking to me was making me sick and driving me crazy! I should have sniffed him to make sure he did not smell like a woman!

When I got to my room, I slammed my door then burst into tears. I laid on my bed with the blanket over my face until I dozed off...

While I was asleep, I was awakened by a sharp pain traveling through the inside of my body. I pulled my covers off then rolled up my sleeves. I had something moving underneath my skin. I screamed out in pain as it burned; I rolled onto the floor drenched in sweat as the pain burned across my back. It felt like hot lava was traveling underneath my skin.

"ARRGGHHHHHHHHHHH!" I screamed out, rolling around on the floor.

Goon burst into my room. "What's the matter? What's going on?" he asked, ripping my clothes off me.

"It hurts so badly! It burns! It fucking burns, ARRGGGHHHHHHHH!" I yelled as the pain sent me sliding into the wall. Goon picked me up then took me into my bathroom. He turned the cold water on then hurriedly stuck me under the showerhead. I could still feel it moving around across my back but it did not burn as much. He stood under the cold water hugging me and rubbing my back.

"It's almost over! Take a deep breath!" he said, holding me.

His rubs were soothing and I almost forgot about the pain until another sharp one came, causing my knees to buckle. I almost collapsed but Goon caught me. We stood under the cold water for what seemed like an hour until he helped me out of the shower. He gave me a towel then walked me in front of the mirror. He handed me a smaller mirror.

"Turn around and hold the mirror up so you can see your back," he said to me. I did what he told me to do then gasped. I had a huge tribal marking covering my entire back! It matched the tattoo that covered Goon's back.

"What is this?" I asked him.

"Instead of wedding rings, we get the same tribal markings. We are now one. We are permanent," he said.

"Is this really real, Goon? We are really soulmates!" I said to him then he walked out of the bathroom.

"Goodnight, Kanya!" he said to me closing my door. I picked up my vase then hurled it at the door.

"ASSHOLE!" I screamed out at him. I put on my jogging suit then headed out of my room.

I walked into the den where Izra sat talking on the phone. He was smiling showing his dimples and his voice was low like he was whispering. I laughed because he was talking dirty to Adika and did not want anyone to hear.

"Tell Adika I'm on my way to her. And I need your car keys," I said to Izra.

"Does Goon know that you are leaving out of the house?" Izra asked me.

"Fuck Goon! Now, where are your keys! I need to get out of this house before I lose my damn mind!" I said to him.

"I will go with you," Izra said.

He just wanted to be under Adika but it did not matter to me as long as I got out of the house. When we headed for the door, Dayo was coming in. He bumped into me then

I shoved him back into the wall. Izra had a scowl on his face and a growl escaped his throat.

"That was some sucka shit! Don't do that again!" Izra said to Dayo. Dayo smirked then headed up the stairs.

"He needs to be exiled from this pack!" Izra said aloud.

Goon walked down the stairs. "Izra! Come talk to me real quick!" Goon's voice boomed throughout the foyer. Izra gave me his car keys then told me he would be right out.

I called Adika while I waited for Izra to come out of the house.

"So, you finally called me back? What time will you be here? I miss you!" she said.

"I been going through a lot. I want to tell you but you might freak out. Goon and I are having problems," I said sadly.

"That's because you both are stubborn. It will get better. I bet the neither of you have actually sat down to try to talk about it. When you get here, we will chat. We are going to have Izra cook dinner for us while we talk," Adika said.

"Is Izra aware of that? I doubt if you will eat the meat if steak is on the menu! Izra and Goon eat theirs somewhat raw!" I laughed.

"He can bake us some fish. Besides, I like a man who can wait on a woman," she replied.

"After he gives you hell about it first! Izra is not the easiest person to talk to!" I said to her. Izra walked out of the house then headed towards his car. When he got in, he looked at me then smirked.

"Adika can fool herself thinking I am cooking for y'all all she wants to! Who does she think she is? I still haven't sniffed her panties yet!" he fussed then I fell over in laughter.

"How do you know what we talked about?" I asked him.

"I was in her head! I have some of Goon's blood in my veins so I can do some of the things he does. I just can't heal as fast," he said to me.

"What were you and Goon talking about?" I asked Izra.

"Just man talk! Damn, you are nosey! I'll be happy when you can listen to his thoughts!" he said.

"Since you are in her head, figure out how many men she slept with then!" I said to him.

"I haven't asked her that question yet, so I can't read her thoughts about it. But I'm asking her tonight after ya'll fix my dinner!" he said. I shook my head because Izra was serious.

Once we got to Adika's apartment, I headed straight to her liquor counter. I needed an escape from my current situation. I found myself confessing my feelings to Goon in my head thinking he would hear them. If he did, he did not respond. It was starting to irk me that I could still smell Xavier's scent on me. I knew that was the real reason why Goon didn't like to be around me. When Xavier was pleasing me with his mouth, he bit me, marking my sex with his scent.

Adika and I chatted in the kitchen while Izra smoked his blunt in the living room. She and I were laughing and joking around but Goon was heavily on my mind. I wanted to know what he was doing and what he was thinking. Even though Adika was talking to me, I was thinking about Goon and I having pups and him impregnating me during the full moon.

"Earth to Kanya!" Adika said.

"Oh, I'm sorry, Adika! I'm just not myself at the moment," I said to her.

"I can see that," she replied. She looked around making sure Izra could not hear what she was about to say. I was sure Izra was listening to her thoughts anyway. There was no type of privacy around Goon and Izra.

"I bought this sexy negligee for Izra. I'm going to finally let him have his way with me tonight," she said and my mouth dropped.

"You are breaking your three-month rule?" I asked her.

"Yes I am! I felt him the other night when we went to the movies. His dick is so big, it's abnormal!" she said with lust in her eyes. If only she knew why he was big! I wanted to tell her but that was against the rules. Izra had to be the one to tell her that he was a werewolf!

"Be careful," I said to her.

After dinner and a few drinks, I had a serious buzz. Adika and Izra were passing sexual glances at each other. He wanted her just as much as she wanted him. His eyes ran along her body as if she was prey and he was ready to attack her. I watched his eyes change color as his beast craved her. I faked a yawn. "Well, it's time for me to go! Izra, I'll take your car home and Adika can drop you off in the morning," I said, grabbing my things. I kissed Adika's cheek then headed out of her door. Izra followed behind me.

"Go straight home, Kanya!" he scolded me.

"Yes, sir! Now, be easy on her! She's human and your beast might be too much for her!" I said to him.

"I can tame my beast!" he said, chuckling then walked back into her building.

The drive back to the mansion was short. I did not take any back roads by the woods; I drove straight through the city. After I parked in the circular driveway, I walked into the house. When I walked into the kitchen, Goon was standing in the middle of the floor drinking a pitcher of water. He must have just gotten back from hunting. He stared at me then I stared back at him sucking my teeth. He laughed at me then walked out of the kitchen. I grabbed my chocolate milk then headed down to my room. After I drank my milk, I flopped down across my bed, my eyelids getting heavy as I drifted off to sleep.

The next morning I woke up topless with just my panties on. I heard the sound of light snores then a growl. I sat up in my bed; Goon was lying next to me. I smiled when I noticed my clothes on the floor. He knows I cannot sleep comfortably with clothes on. I like to sleep with just my panties on or naked. I stared into his handsome face then traced the markings on his back as he slept on his stomach. I pulled the covers back and noticed that he was naked also. I inhaled his scent; my nipples hardened and a strong ache formed between my legs.

"GOON!" I called out to him.

"In the morning, Kanya! I'm tired!" he spat angrily. He hated to be disturbed while sleeping.

"I thought you were mad at me," I said to him.

"I can't sleep without you. I haven't been to sleep in a week and I couldn't take it anymore," he said, falling back to sleep. I shook him and even bit his ear but he did not budge. I was sexually frustrated!

It had been three days and Goon was still asleep! I did everything to wake him up and he would not budge! He had been in my bed for three days straight.

"KOFFFIIIIIIIII!" I screamed out. Moments later, he came running down the stairs.

"What's the matter?" Kofi asked me.

"I think he's dead! He won't wake up!" I said to him.

"Goon sleeps like that when he doesn't get any sleep. One time he slept for a week straight. But when he wakes up, he will have an appetite of five starving wolves," Kofi said.

SOUL Publications

Amadi came downstairs with some type of ancient-looking gold urn. Amadi reminded me of Tyson Beckford the male model, he looks almost identical to him. Amadi even had the same build as him. Kofi also resembled an actor by the name of Dijmon Hounsou, same complexion and all.

"What is that?" I asked Amadi.

"A remedy that I have been making for the past week. You have to soak in it for four hours to get Xavier's scent off you. I can smell it now and it's driving us all crazy," Amadi said, giving me the urn.

"It doesn't go away on its own?" I asked them.

"Yes, once Goon puts his scent back on you but since you smell like another wolf, his sexual desires for you don't exist. He will not make love to you if you smell like a male wolf even if it's the only way he can get rid of it!" Kofi said.

"In other words, Goon can't get an erection to pleasure you. Xavier knew what he was doing so Goon would not mate with you. Damn, I want to rip his throat apart!" Amadi said with his eyes changing colors. I could feel the heat radiate off his body, he was getting angry. I was starting to feel embarrassed that the other wolves knew Xavier gave me pleasure. I put my head down but Kofi lifted my chin up.

"Don't feel ashamed! Sometimes our bodies give in, even when we don't want it to! My mate was raped centuries and centuries ago by a clan of wolves who could not resist her scent. She had pleasure from it because she was in heat. I knew in my soul that I was the only one for her," Kofi said to me.

"God that is awful! I'm sorry you had to go through that," I said, wiping my eyes then hugged him.

After they left my room, I grabbed my robe, my cellphone and iPod. I went to the kitchen then grabbed two bottles of wine. I went to the gym room and then ran the water in the hot tub getting it as hot as I could tolerate it. I dumped the thick brown, oily, sticky substance into the water. I slipped all the way in preparing for my four hours of soaking. I called my parents and Adika; Sasha left me a message but I ignored it. I sipped my wine from the bottle as I listened to Jill Scott on my iPod. Her music was soothing and calming; Amadi could be a millionaire if he sold his remedies. The oil made my skin smooth and radiant!

Goon

*T*he sun beamed on my face when Kanya opened the curtains, causing me to hold my hand up in front of my face. My stomach growled; I felt like I had not eaten in years! I could go for a whole cow right now.

"Good morning, handsome!" Kanya greeted me, kissing my lips. I sniffed the air and her welcoming scent tingled my nose.

"His scent is gone!" I said, getting out of the bed. She turned on the water to take a shower then took her clothes off. I brushed my teeth before I got into the shower with her.

"How long was I asleep for?" I asked her while she washed my chest.

"Five days," she replied.

Her eyes latched onto mine, giving me a pleading look. "I've been acting out. I apologize for that," I said to her.

She hugged me. "I missed you!" she said, holding on to me. She was getting stronger and more comfortable with her beast.

"I can't breathe, girl! You are squeezing the fuck out of me!" I said to her then she blushed. After I rinsed my body off, I washed her back; I traced her tattoo on her back with my finger.

SOUL Publications

"As good as my tattoo looks on your body, I'm still mad that you had to endure the pain. This is just the beginning of it. You will get more and they will only get worse," I told her.

"If it's meant to be, it's meant to be. Now when can we go baby shopping?" she asked me then I roared in laughter.

"You are serious, huh?" I asked her.

"Yes, I am! I want you to meet my parents as well," she said to me.

"Okay, cool. You have to teach me what to do around them. Humans have too many rules for everything," I said to her.

"Watch it!" she said.

Kanya grabbed at my dick with her soapy hands. She started to massage me from my testicles to the head of my shaft. She squeezed my testicles with her right hand as she jerked me off with her other hand.

"What are you doing?" I asked her almost growling.

"I'm jerking you off," she said to me. I had never experienced this before! When I have sex, it was always about me just pleasing the woman, which is in our wolf nature.

"SHIT!" I growled as her small hands wrapped around my girth, gently squeezing it. Up and down, round and round she went. She lowered down onto her knees in the shower; she took me into her warm and wet mouth. I grabbed the shower rod as Kanya shoved my dick down her throat as she continued to massage me. Something in me was telling me to grip her hair, which I did to steady her movements. She looked up at me with gold eyes and her nails grew out.

"Don't scratch me, Kanya!" I growled, she growled back at me putting me further into her mouth.

I did not know a woman's throat could expand that wide! She popped me out of her mouth then flicked her tongue across the tip of my shaft. I almost moaned aloud sounding like a woman! She slid her hand down her lower stomach, spreading her sex open. Her middle finger entered the small tight hole that makes my beast go insane. She moved her finger in and out of herself. She moaned on my dick, sending a sensation so strong through my body that I was light-headed. My dick swelled up then she slid me further down her throat. She moaned as she pleased herself and me.

"ARRGGGGGHHHHHHHHHH!" I released myself into her mouth as I pumped harder down her throat.

"What did you do with that?" I asked her.

"I swallowed it, Goon," she said. Her scent filled the bathroom and I wanted to take her but I needed to eat. I was starving and when I starve, I become aggressive.

I hurriedly rinsed off again then got out of the shower. I wrapped a towel around my waist then practically ran to the fridge that was built into the wall in our kitchen. That is where we kept our fresh meat after we hunted it. When I opened up the door, there was a small steak sitting on the shelf. I grabbed it then stuffed it into my mouth; it made my stomach ache even more from hunger. I went into the other fridge and it was empty! I knocked the fridge over; Kanya ran into the kitchen fully dressed.

"What's the matter? Why are you making all of this noise?" she asked me.

"I'm starving!" I told her.

"Walk around the back of the house with me," Kanya told me.

"I'm not in the mood right now! I need to eat first! Show me later!" I said, getting ready to shift.

"Can you just listen to me? Walk around the back of the house with me!" she said.

I growled as I followed her thinking of a juicy pregnant deer. I could even go for an Ox right now! I followed Kanya outside around the back of the house. There was a cow hooked to the fence in the backyard.

"I wanted to surprise you!" she said, kissing my lips.

"Let me thank you later, baby! I need to eat!" I said dropping my towel as I shifted.

I charged into the cow ripping its neck apart. Kanya covered her mouth as she watched me take down the large animal. After I was done feasting, I went for a run to burn some of my meal off. Amadi and Elle butchered the rest of the cow for some of its meat for later. When I got back to the house, I showered again before I got dressed.

"Where are you going?" Kanya eyed me.

"We are going out, so get dolled up," I said, smirking. She hurriedly went to her room to get dressed.

Izra looked at me chuckling. "You feeling better now, nigga?" he asked me.

"Brand-new, bro!" I laughed.

"He must've got some!" Elle said laughing.

Dayo rolled his eyes at me the way Kanya does. I had not said a word to him since the dream he had about me. I had been avoiding him and did not stay in the same room as him longer than five minutes.

"Nigga, what the fuck are you over there acting like a diva for? I am tired of this nigga! Damn, the only female that should be in this house is Kanya! Kofi, you need to check him!" Izra yelled out.

"Can you just shut up, Izra? And stop messing with him! He is still our brother!" Elle said, defending Dayo.

"I'm out of here!" Izra said, getting mad and walked out of the house. Kanya came back downstairs dressed in tight pants, a fitted sweater and high-heels. I loved when she wore those types of shoes; it made her walk more seductive with her hips swaying side to side. Her hair has grown out, now she styled it in an edgy short cut with tresses falling down into her face.

"The lady and I are staying out tonight. I will see y'all tomorrow," I said to the pack. They gave me the head nod, but Dayo stormed out of the room like a jealous Alpha female. Kanya chuckled then switched down the hall towards the door. Her ass was getting more plump and fuller; her thighs and curves spread more, giving her pup-bearing hips.

"Bite me, baby!" she said over her shoulder.

"Oh, I will!" I said, hugging her from the back. I sniffed her neck then licked it making her moan. I opened up the truck door for her, helping her get in. When I got inside, I started the truck then pulled off.

"Where are we going?" she asked me.

"The Poconos Mountains, I have a cabin up there that no one knows about. I like to get away from the pack every now and then. There is more food there and the woods remind me of the visions I have of my past life," I told her.

"We can always go back when we have the pups. Just us up in the mountains away from civilization," Kanya said.

"You still have human ways. You like to party, hangout with your friends, go shopping and all of that other stuff you are into doing. I can't take that away from you," I said to her.

"I can't just think of myself anymore. It's no longer just about me," she said, grabbing my hand.

"Your words always make me feel mushy," I said laughing.

"Oh, no! Not the big black beast!" she said, squeezing my cheek.

Xavier

*T*wo of my pack brothers' bodies were burned after we had their ceremony. Ismal and Jonah were twin brothers that had joined the pack just recently. Goon tore them to shreds! My father was telling the truth about the gods being upset because we were not healing at all. Amilia was on bed rest with an old witch doctor nursing her wounds. Kanya almost killed her! Seeing Kanya turned into a gold jackal made me crave her even more. Her taste was still on the tip of my tongue. My father gave me the name of a witch who had a cure for our wounds to help them heal faster. She lived deep in the woods and it took hours traveling in wolf form just to reach her. Even in wolf form we moved slower because of our wounds.

"Is this it?" Aki asked in my head.

"It should be," I said to him.

"You sure, this doesn't look creepy enough. I thought witch houses looked haunted," Aki said chuckling.

"Let's get this over with," I said.

When I got in front of the door, it opened, and Aki followed behind me. There were potion bottles and candles everywhere. She had hieroglyphics all over the walls. *This must be the place where she practices all of her magic and spells. There's even a voodoo doll in the middle of the table and it appears to be a woman,* I thought to myself.

"Who is there?" she called out. I howled then she came out of the back room. Aki and I were still in wolf form; in human form, our wounds were painfully intolerable!

"What do you seek here?" the witch asked me.

"We need a cure," I said through my mind. Witches could read anyone's minds, dreams, and even sometimes predict the future. They were very magical creatures but could be more dangerous when they were evil.

Her long locks dragged the floor and the gold bracelets jingled around her ankles; she was topless. Her hair covered her breasts and she wore a thin, sheer, gold wraparound long skirt. The way her hips swayed when she walked, she could have been some type of dancer. Her skin was smooth and dark, the color of a Hershey's bar. She was beautiful!

"Are you Keora?" I asked her.

"Yes, I am. I know all about you. I know why you are here. What makes you think I would help you?" she asked with a smirk on her face. Aki dropped a diamond bracelet onto the floor from out of his mouth. She picked it up then examined it, before tossing it back at Aki. "It's not expensive enough for my taste. You may go now," she stated.

I growled at her. "What's the matter? The big bad wolf is going to blow my house down?" she said then laughed loudly making the window shutters fly open.

"You are going to regret this!" I said.

"There is only one wolf that makes me tingle and that's the prince, Goon! Now get out of my home before I make a nice coat out of the both of you! You are getting fleas everywhere!" she snapped.

I leaped into her. *"Find the potion!"* I said to Aki in his head. I sank my teeth into Keora's neck; she used a powerful force, knocking me into the wall. The wounds on her neck closed up. Her eyes were now pitch-black; her dreads grew out longer before she grabbed me by the neck, slamming me into the wall. Some of her hair tried to reach for Aki but he dodged her. I clawed her hair, shredding it away from my neck.

They said the best way to get a witch is to sneak them from the back. I climbed up the wall then onto the ceiling. She was distracted by Aki when I jumped behind her, then sank my teeth into the back of her neck. She reached back scratching at my face. I bit her hand and blood squirted inside my mouth. Her hair reached for me again like long, skinny snakes snapping at me but I dodged them. I sank my teeth further into her neck.

"Found it!" Aki said, running out of the house. Someone flew into the window landing on their feet. I sniffed the air and the scent reminded me of one of the wolves in Goon's pack. Black's eyes stared at me; she resembled Keora but was more beautiful. Her hair dragged the ground as well.

"Let my sister go!" she said her long, black, pointy nails growing to the size of kitchen knives.

I dragged Keora towards the door using her as a shield. The other witch had the scent of a wolf! I looked into her face and that is when I realized who she was—Kanya's friend Adika. Adika spun around then turned into an over-sized black Mau. I dropped Keora then leaped out the door, jumping into the trees; Aki was already long gone. Adika leaped up into the tree then chased after me as I jumped from tree to tree. I saw a river then dived in it because cats do not like water. When I got on the other side, she stood on the opposite side watching me.

"You cursed your family!" she said in my head.

"Fuck you!" I said then took off running in the woods. I know deep down I was in deep shit but Kanya's scent was worth it all!

When I finally made it back to my home, Amilia was lying in bed with bandages wrapped around her body and face. Unlike other Alphas, Amilia was picked by my father and her father. We were not mating by fate and I held a re-sentment towards her because of it. I was forcing myself to love her, and the more I tried the more I hated her. I sat the water down next to her then left back out of the room.

Aki and I split the potion; I did not want anyone else besides us to know about it. The other wolves were still wounded, staying in their wolf form in order to cope with the pain. Aki went to his room down the hall. The other wolves had their rooms in the basement. In our species, the pack lives together.

When I went back to the room, Amilia was eyeing me with a scowl on her face. "What is it now? And I hope it's worthy of my time because I have somewhere to be!" I told her.

"I still can't believe you tried to mark another wolf! Even after I followed you and saw it with my own eyes, you still act unbothered!" Amila screamed at me.

"And time and time again, we always end this conversation with me walking out the door! Are you mad? Take it up with our fathers since the treaty voted for you and I to mate! I don't even know if I want to have pups with you. I don't even want to screw you. However, I will to keep my father happy. And if you want your father to remain happy, let's pretend we are the happiest fucking couple," I said to her. She burst out in tears.

"She doesn't even want you! She wants Goon! He is stronger, more powerful, and he is the son of Ammon! You aren't nothing but a punk who hides behind his pack! You are a coward! I bet his dick is bigger than yours! I know it is because Kanya's hips have swelled! You know what that means, don't you?" Amilia spat.

I leaped onto the bed, choking her. "I will kill you!" I said as she scratched at my arm. Lance ran into the room pushing me off Amilia. Dash stood in the doorway with a cocky grin on his face. Everyone was injured from the fight in the woods, all except for Dash. He was not even there and, matter of fact, he had been missing for over a week.

"Look who decided to show up!" I said, taunting him. He looked at Amilia and his eyes softened. I always had a gut feeling that they were having an affair behind my back. Amilia put her head down and I slapped her. "You never bow your head down to another wolf who isn't an Alpha!" I said to her.

"I hope Goon tears you to shreds like a stuffed animal! Oh, wait I forgot, he already did!" she said, standing up to me.

I stormed out of the bedroom as she yelled and screamed obscenities. I went to the spare bedroom I slept in to shower and get dressed. My wounds were closing up already because of the potion I stole from Keora. After I put my clothes on, Aki, Lance and I headed to the club. It was ladies night tonight and I had to make sure the bar was stocked and the DJ played the right music that would get the crowd rowdy. Aki and Lance were the bodyguards. Lance was still wounded, but his wounds had stopped bleeding. He moved slower than usual and I knew he wanted to shift to wolf form to subside the pain but he could not because of club duty.

When I walked in Club Fangz the music was blaring and the ladies all flocked to me. They knew my dad was rich and that I reaped the benefits of it. I flirted with a few but none of them piqued my interest.

"Hey, Xavier! We have a new bartender!" Joseph, the manager, said to me.

"Bring her to me. Is she dark meat?" I asked him. It was not a secret that I was attracted to black women. There was something sexual about them that I enjoyed. Their voluptuous curves, full breasts and nice plump ass!

Joseph laughed then told me to follow him. When I got to my office that overlooked the club, the new bartender was sitting in the chair. She was an ebony beauty! Her hair was cut short; her eyes big and slightly slanted. Her lips were full and her cheekbones high and perfectly sculpted. She stood up and my mouth hit the floor. Her curves were outrageous! I sniffed the air and her scent was enticing. A growl slipped from my throat as I tried to contain myself. I wanted to rip her short black skirt off and bend her over! My penis hardened against my slacks. I needed her and I was going to have her.

"Joseph, let me get acquainted with the new bartender," I told him. He nodded his head then walked out of my office, shutting the door.

"Have a seat. I'm sorry I didn't catch your name…" I said.

She smiled. "My name is Naobi," she said in a strong accent.

"Pretty name! It matches your face. Where are you from?" I asked her.

"I'm from Africa," she said, crossing her long, lean, shiny legs. Her breasts were popping out of her button-up shirt. I caught a glimpse of her black lace bra.

"Is this the way you treat all women, Xavier? My face is up here, not below my chin. Now that you know my name and where I am from, you can show me around," she said in a demanding tone.

"We can wait. I want to know you more. So, do you have any kids, perhaps a husband?" I asked her.

"I have a son. And, yes, my husband and I have been together for a very long time," she said to me. I really did not care, I just wanted to taste and penetrate her. She seductively walked to the door. "I understand I will be filling the last bartender's spot," she said to me.

"Yes, you will be. Kanya was good at what she did. I hope you are as good as her, maybe even better," I said, walking towards her.

"Kanya? Beautiful name. Her name means *beautiful*. I can see that you were smitten with her," Naobi said in her thick accent.

"She is a down to earth person," I said, opening the door.

"I bet she is! She sounds like she can make a man happy. A strong and powerful man. Women like her are made for those types of men," she said then walked out of the door as I held it open. I did not like the sound of that! Was it possible that she knew Kanya?

As she walked in front of me, I decided to get into her head but there was a problem…a huge problem! Her mind was blocked!

Who is this woman? I asked myself.

SOUL Publications

Kanya

"**C**atch the fish!" I screamed, jumping up and down. We had been in the mountains for a whole day now. Goon was standing in the lake shirtless with his pants rolled up. He was bending down trying to catch the fish with his bare hands.

"You have to be patient, Kanya," he said in his deep soothing voice. Once a big fish swam through his legs, he caught it, sinking his nails into the fish instantly killing it.

"That was really gross!" I said. Goon and I were not going to eat the fish. It was bait, so that he could catch a black bear for dinner.

Goon's appetite is outrageous. I can imagine if he was human, the grocery tab would be very expensive, I thought to myself.

"I'm not that greedy, Kanya," he laughed, throwing the fish in the basket with the rest of the dead fish.

"I wish you would stop reading my mind! Damn it, Goon! I have no privacy around you! Not even when I'm on the toilet!" I said to him.

"Your human ways of thinking entertain me! Plus, it connects me to your soul even more," he said, towering over me.

A Beauty to His Beast: An Urban Werewolf Story   Natavia

"You just wait until I can pop up in your mind whenever I feel like it," I said then he shrugged.

"That will just make you aroused. The thoughts I have of you are very explicit," he said and I pinched him.

Goon picked up the big heavy basket with the dead fish then threw me over his shoulder like a feather.

"Let me go!" I giggled. He sank his canines into my right ass cheek. Wetness seeped from my slit; I could hear Goon sniffing then he groaned.

"You are such an animal!" I said.

Once we got to the log cabin, he spread all of the fish around the house to draw in the bears. Afterwards, we took a shower then headed to the fireplace. Goon was walking around naked showing all of his tribal markings. He brought me a glass of wine then sat down beside me.

"Are you still mad about who you really are?" Goon asked, staring into my eyes.

"I was at first because it scared the heck out of me. I thought I was going crazy! I thought you were crazy! After I accepted it, I had peace of mind. It is beautiful to be able to connect to someone spiritually! I feel so alive!" I said to him.

I sat my wine glass down then leaned over to kiss his lips. I slipped my tongue into his mouth; he hungrily sucked on it. He opened my robe and groped my breast. His hands were like magic and every time he touched me, my body burned with an insatiable desire. A strong ache formed between my legs, causing me to whine. He captured my swollen nipple between his teeth, a mannish-animalistic growl echoed throughout the small cabin. He gripped the back of my head pulling it back to expose my neck. After he sucked my nipples, he placed soft sensual kisses on my neck.

"GOONNNNN!" I whined. My body temperature started to rise. My canines pierced through my gums, my nails through my skin.

"You want me to fuck you, don't you?" he asked me, his eyes turning blue. Wetness poured from between my lips onto the wooden floors. He was right, I did not want the slow lovemaking like I normally did, I wanted his beast! I wanted him to make me surrender! I wanted him to take charge, like the beast I knew he was born to be.

I got down on all fours, arching my back as high as I could arch it. My upper body was flat down on the cold floor. He opened me up, sticking his nose inside of me then he howled. His long, wet tongue entered me, causing me to moan out in pleasure. His soft wet and full lips sucked on my hole, his teeth gently nibbling my clit.

"Baby, please stick it in further!" I moaned. He separated my lips further apart then kissed my dripping hole. His tongue snaked around inside of me, making my body tremble. I winced in pain when his sharp nails went into my ass cheeks. *"Keep still!"* he demanded.

The slurping sounds of my wetness filled the cabin. My essence poured out of me like faucet water, splashing onto the floor. Goon had me soaking wet. My pussy pulsated, bringing me into a head-spinning climax. As I tried to catch my breath, I let out a long gasp. Goon's oversized dick was penetrating me. He pinned me down between him

SOUL Publications

and the floor. I could not move as I laid stuck; his girth stretched me open, coming to a hilt that made me scream. My nails scratched the floor as he worked himself inside me.

He smacked my ass. "Please me!" he demanded, smacking it again harder. I could feel the new scratches opening up on my skin where he smacked me. He raised up, so I could move my hips.

"GGRRRRRRR! UMMMMMMMM!" he moaned as I threw my backside against his pelvis. He bucked backed, causing his dick to go further into me.

"I feel it in my stomach! Goon, it hurts!" I cried out as he stretched me open wider.

"Spread your legs and relax!" he said into my head. I spread my legs wider with my butt further up into the air. Goon gripped both cheeks then slowly pushed in and out of me. He grinded inside me, pulled out then left the tip in, giving me a long hard thrust that hit my spot causing me to howl. My body collapsed onto the floor as I lost control of my legs. I was having the biggest orgasm I ever received. His veins thickened in his dick then it hardened. He jabbed into my spot over and over again.

"Fuck me back! Squeeze my dick, Kanya!" he growled, going deeper. I honestly could not fuck him back! He was too deep, too powerful and too strong. I wanted it this way! I wanted him to take my body with no limits. I wanted him to pound every drop out of my pussy until I screamed mercy!

He chuckled. "You like when I take advantage of you, huh?" he asked, going harder and deeper inside of me.

"YESSSSSSSSSS! RIGHT THERE!" I clawed at the floor, trembling from another orgasm. Goon let out a loud growl that sounded like he was wounded. I felt his semen shoot up into me like a water hose. He collapsed on top of my sweaty body. He tried to pull out of me but he was stuck. "WHAT THE FUCK!" he yelled out.

"Don't yank it out!" I said.

"Kanya, my dick is stuck inside of you!" he fussed.

"Isn't that what happens when dogs mate? The male's penis swells and pumps semen into the female until she gets pregnant?" I asked him.

"Don't refer to us as dogs! We do not have owners nor do we beg for treats! Besides, you and I are not mating! Although you are in heat, it is still not a full moon!" he fussed. I released him then fell over laughing.

"You pranked me!" he growled.

"Whew! It took many muscles for that to happen. I saw two dogs get stuck after breeding years ago and I thought since you and I are like dogs, we could laugh about it!" I said laughing with tears in my eyes.

I heard a grumble outside. "It's a bear out there! I can smell him!" Goon said.

"What do we do?" I asked him.

"We eat him!" he said. I did not mind eating the meat after someone chopped it up for me. However, for me to eat it straight out of the animal made my stomach turn.

A Beauty to His Beast: An Urban Werewolf Story   Natavia

He shifted right before my eyes; he looked at me with his blue eyes and menacing stare. I shifted into my beast form; Goon licked my face then rubbed his head against mine. I snapped my teeth at him playfully. Goon ran across the floor in full speed then jumped through the window. The sounds of glass breaking and loud growling rang through my sensitive ears. I ran then leaped out of the window behind him. The bear Goon was wrestling was huge! Its claws were sharp and long and so were its teeth. The bear stood up on its hind legs, overshadowing Goon. Goon's ears went back as he crouched down licking his sharp canines. The bear let out a threating growl as Goon charged into the oversized beast. The bear clawed at Goon as Goon's sharp teeth pierced through the bear's neck. Blood splattered on the ground, the bear swatted at Goon's face. I climbed up a tree then leaped onto the bear's back when it rolled over on top of Goon. I aimed for its neck, sinking my teeth into it. The fresh taste of blood made me want to kill. My stomach growled as I thought about my heavy meal. Goon bit into the other side of the bear's neck. The bear tried to fight us off but it was getting weak and collapsed onto the ground. When he stopped breathing, Goon tore into its stomach like a wild animal. He pulled a chunk out of its stomach then dropped it on the ground next to me. I devoured the thick, bloody, raw and chewy meat. My stomach growled for more and Goon gave it to me. When we got back into the cabin, we were bloody. Goon and I headed straight for the shower then got into bed.

"I'm stuffed," he said.

"Me, too," I said, cuddling underneath him.

SOUL Publications

A Beauty to His Beast: An Urban Werewolf Story   Natavia

We stayed up in the mountains for a few more days before heading home. The bear we killed still had a lot of meat left on it so Goon butchered it making steaks out of it. He was giving it to his pack brothers. When I got back home, I called Adika. When she answered the phone, she sounded sad.

"What's the matter with you?" I asked her.

"I told Izra I couldn't see him again," she said.

"WHAT! Why would you do that? I thought you two were getting along," I said to her.

"We were but he and I are so different, Kanya!" she sniffled into the phone.

"I will be over, so we can talk about it then," I said to her. After I hung up with Adika, I headed back upstairs. I walked into the kitchen and Kofi was cutting up a piece of meat.

"There's my beautiful jackal! How was your little getaway? I see the mean beast is in a good mood! I have never seen that pup smile so much!" Kofi said joyfully.

"It was fun and relaxing. I'm just trying to get used to being a nature woman," I said, kissing his cheek then he blushed.

"Where are Elle, Izra and Amadi?" I asked Kofi.

"They took Izra out of the house! That girl he was seeing told him she did not want to talk to him anymore. Izra did not like that too much. Wolves are territorial! When

Izra laid down with her, she became his," Kofi said, chewing the meat.

"He marked her?" I asked Kofi.

"Yes, he marked her then she told him she didn't want to be bothered. She's a human, so once she says that, she does not have to deal with him. If she were a wolf she wouldn't have a choice! I keep telling the pack to never give in to their desire for humans!" Kofi stated. After Kofi and I chatted, I showered then changed my clothes. I walked into my room with just a towel wrapped around my body. I went into my walk-in closet to get out some clothes to wear.

"Where are you going?" Goon's voice boomed from behind me.

"I'm going to see Adika and we might go out. Is that okay with you? How do you like this outfit?" I turned around. holding the shirt and pants together. Goon had a displeased look etched on his face. "I don't like it. It seems as if it would show too much," he said.

"Why did you buy it?" I asked him laughing but he was not laughing with me. He crossed his arms then leaned against the closet doorway.

"Your hips have spread since then! Your breasts will pop out of that shirt!" he spat. I rolled my eyes then picked out a longer top.

"You can't just roam around freely!" he said to me.

"Don't start it, Goon!" I yelled at him. His eyes changed color indicating that I pissed off his beast. "You are not capable of fighting off another wolf, Kanya! You are still in heat!" he yelled at me.

"I am not a fucking baby!" I gave him the same tone he gave me.

"Okay, cool! Let's see how big and bad you are when you are put in another position like before!" he said walking out of the room.

"Go to hell!" I screamed out. I ripped the clothes that I had in my hands to shreds.

"GREAT! I didn't mean to do that," I said to myself. I picked out another outfit then got dressed. I grabbed Goon's truck keys, my purse and cell-phone. I headed towards the door.

"Be safe!" Goon said to me. I looked him up and down and he was dressed casually. He had on a pair of jeans, Timbs, and a sweater that hugged his chest but was not too tight. The sweater fit him perfectly! He wore a diamond chain necklace around his neck. I growled at him then he chuckled.

"Where are you going?" I asked him, becoming jealous.

"I'm getting ready to meet my brothers!" he said, walking past me. His cologne tickled my nose; my sex pulsated as I eyed him. He was so mannish and beautiful! His strong unique features caused him to stand out more than any man I had ever encountered. My heart beat faster as I thought about how I was made just for him.

SOUL Publications

"I don't want you to go anywhere!" I called out to him. He turned around with his body towering over mine. He looked into my eyes.

"And why is that?" he chuckled.

"Can you wear a sweat suit and wash that cologne off?" I asked him. The thought of women flocking to him was sending me over the edge.

"No, I'm not changing a damn thing, Kanya! I am going to have a few drinks and unwind! You want to have your fun and so do I!" he said, walking down the driveway towards a black Dodge Charger.

"Can I have a kiss?" I asked him pouting. Goon had officially spoiled me! I hated it and loved it all at the same time.

Goon chuckled then turned around with his arms spread, licking his lips. I wanted him to take me right there and now but I had just texted Adika, telling her that I was on my way. When I got to him, I threw my arms around his neck; he bent down capturing my lips. A moan escaped my throat when he lifted me up then held me against his truck. I wrapped my legs around his waist as his tongue slid down my throat.

"UMMMMM!" I moaned as his hard-on pressed against my center.
"I want to slide into you so badly!" he whispered in my ear, caressing my nipples through my blouse.

Goon's strength was causing my body to put a dent into the side of his truck. I felt the metal caving in as he pressed his body firmly against mine.

SOUL Publications

"I need it!" I moaned, massaging his shaft through his jeans. He was long, thick and hard; he wanted me just as bad. Sweat beads formed on my forehead as I anticipated his next move.

"I've got to go check up on Izra," he said, putting me down, leaving me panting and throbbing.

"Where they at?" I asked him then he smirked.

"Strip club," he said.

"Oh, hell no!" I said to him. He chuckled then disappeared.

I never saw him disappear like that before; I looked around then all of a sudden, the Charger zoomed out of the driveway.

"Have fun!" he said, laughing inside my head.

When I got to Adika's apartment, I was livid. Goon being with Izra at a strip club was not doing me any good. I slammed my purse down on her table.

"What's the matter with you?" she asked me.

"Goon is gone with Izra to a strip club! I hope he doesn't grab anyone's ass!" I said to Adika.

"Ohhhhh, you are jealous!" she said, putting on her pumps. I noticed something different about Adika. I had not seen her since the day Izra brought me over to her home. Her hips were wider, her breasts fuller. He definitely marked her!

"Let's get drunk tonight!" she said to me. Adika was acting weird. Very weird and I could not put my finger on it but she seemed a little off.

"What's the matter with you?" I asked her then she burst into tears. I rubbed her back as she sobbed.

"I just want to be normal!" she cried.

"Huh?" I asked her.

"I've been trying to live my life like a normal person. I was fine until I had to reveal myself. I cannot give Izra what he needs. It is impossible. But I really do like him," she said, wiping her eyes.

"You are scaring me, Adika! What the hell is going on with you? Talk to me," I said to her.

"I'm a witch, Kanya," she said, dropping a bomb on me.

"A witch?" I asked in disbelief. Then again I shouldn't be surprised because I was a jackal and Goon was an ancient wolf prince! Yeah, nothing was unbelievable at this point!

"I'm a witch shifter! I can shift to any animal I desire. I have a sister that can shift to any person she chooses. We were born from spells. We came out of the ground. We are created from magic. I know Izra is a werewolf! I know everything! Goon's mother created my sister and me," she said.

"You knew all along?" I asked her.

"Yes, but I couldn't bring myself to tell you. All I ever wanted was to be normal. I wanted a real friend and a real boyfriend. But in reality, I can never have those things," she said, wiping her eyes.

"Yes, you can! Being what you are doesn't determine your happiness," I said to her then she smiled.

"What would Izra think?" she asked me.

"He couldn't tell you're immortal?" I asked her.

"Witches don't have scents! Our identity is secret until we reveal ourselves," she said to me.

"My best friend is a witch. I'm a jackal and my soul-mate is a wolf! Can we have that drink now?" I asked then she laughed. She snapped her fingers and a big bottle of wine and two glasses appeared in front of me.

"Drink up until I finish my make-up!" she laughed, heading towards her bathroom.

"I need something to smoke also!" I called out to her. A blunt appeared between my lips. "I couldn't ask for a better friend!" I said to her.

After I parked Goon's truck, Adika and I got out heading to the long line in front of the club.

"My sister is here!" Adika said to me.

SOUL Publications

"Adika!" someone called out. When I turned around, it was the same girl who was asking Goon for directions. I rolled my eyes at Adika's sister. I had always known Adika had a sister but over the years, I had never met her. Adika told me that her sister lived in another state.

"What's the matter with you?" Adika asked me.

"Nothing," I said as her sister laughed.

"Smile now my child!" her sister said in Mrs. Carroll's voice then Adika laughed.

"You've met her already? This is Keora," Adika introduced.

"You got me fired!" I said, laughing.

"Your Alpha got you fired! He gave me a nice piece of jewelry because of it; I did not mind helping out. I was tired of being that old woman with a shitty caregiver. Sasha almost made me turn her into a pile of shit," Keora said.

"Are you two disguised now?" I asked them.

"Not me! I can only change my hair. Keora is disguised as always!" Adika said.

After we went into the club, we talked and danced. I had a slight buzz. I noticed Keora and Adika started whispering and pointing by the door. Xavier walked in with his pack. I started to panic and beads of sweat formed on my forehead. *How does he always find me?* I wondered.

"That asshole!" Keora spat.

"You know him?" I asked her. She and Adika told me what happened between them and Xavier at Keora's home. I could not believe the lengths Xavier was willing to take his pack through to get to me. Adika also told me that Xavier was the reason she dumped Izra. She let Xavier see her as a witch and she was afraid he would blow her cover.

"I was going to put a spell on him and his whole pack but someone else is taking care of it. She told me not to worry and that it was time for her to step in. I cannot overstep her commands! So, if she wants me to back off, that shall be!" Adika said. I was ready to respond when I heard Xavier's annoying voice.

"Well, well look at what we have here," Xavier said, sniffing my neck. I growled at him then he chuckled. "Cute, very cute! You do know this is my newest club, don't you? We bought it yesterday! This is my territory now!" Xavier said to me. The other wolves with him growled at us as their pupils changed. Xavier used to be attractive to me; he resembled Channing Tatum in a way. He had a few tattoos on his arms and around his neck. If you close your eyes and talk to him, you would not think he was white.

Xavier looked at Adika then smiled. "Meow!" he said, laughing at her. He looked at Keora. "I like this college girl look better on you," he said, caressing her cheek. His body flew across the dance floor crashing down onto the bar counter. Keora laughed then sipped her drink. *How did she do that?* I wondered.

"These are different wolves! Xavier is building up his pack! Goon and his pack will be outnumbered!" Adika said in my head.

"Wait a minute! You can pop up in my head, too?" I asked her.

"Only when I'm close to you. It's a witch thing," she answered.

"I need to leave," I said to them, getting up. Xavier appeared in front of me smiling.

"The potion he stole from Keora made him stronger and faster!" Adika's voice boomed in my head. The other wolves circled around me then I took off running through the crowd. When I got outside to the parking lot, I shifted into my beast. I crept along the cars and waited for Xavier to come out. The doors burst open and growls could be heard. It was only us outside in the empty parking lot.

"Where's Lassie?" Xavier called out to me, as the rest of his pack laughed. I felt a presence next to me. When I looked beside me, it was a black and grey spotted, oversized cat that resembled a panther. The only difference was that the cat was narrow in structure and had a pointy face with pointy ears.

"It's me!" Adika said in my head.

"Beautiful!" I said, admiring Adika's beast.

Adika and I crept along the cars until we were behind them. Xavier's pack shifted, we were outnumbered! It was only Adika and me against the four of them. When I got a clear view of Xavier, I ran then jumped on him. I sank my teeth into his neck. Adika leaped on one of the wolves clawing at their eyes.

Keora landed out of the sky with long dreaded hair that moved around like snakes. Xavier and I rolled around biting and clawing each other. He was bigger and stronger than I was and slung me into a car causing the windows to shatter out. I was injured and bleeding. He charged into me…

SOUL Publications

Goon

"**N**o more shots, Izra!" I said to him over the loud music. A dark-skinned busty stripper danced in his lap while he slapped her ass cheeks.

Amadi and Elle threw money at the stripper as she entertained Izra. When the music went off, she picked up her money then left our section. I sipped my smooth cognac straight listening to the rap music they played throughout the club.

"I think I need another round. This one is on me!" Izra said over the music. Amadi and Elle cheered him on but I did not.

"You need to cut this shit out, Izra," I said to him. When Izra drank too much, he shifted anywhere!

"I almost bit her head off when she told me she didn't want to see me anymore! She also said that we needed to date people of our own kind! What the hell does that mean? She is black and so am I! What the hell did she mean by that?" Izra asked confused.

"Why did you mark her? She's human!" I said to Izra.

"We were fucking and it felt too good! I bit her! I couldn't help it!" Izra said.

"You bit a human and didn't kill her? What wolf have you ever known to bite a human and not kill them? Those marking bites are vicious!" I said to him. Amadi and Elle looked at Izra waiting for his answer.

"Maybe she isn't human! I bit a woman once, two hundred years ago! I killed her because she bled to death! I haven't slept with a human since!" Amadi said.

"Nigga, you haven't slept with a woman period since then! I know about that freaky shit you be watching, while you think everyone is gone hunting!" Izra said, making us laugh. Amadi growled at Izra and we laughed even harder.

"Dayo has been quiet lately," Elle said to us.

"I'm in a strip club with nothing but titties and ass and you bring up Dayo? My dick just went limp!" Izra said, shaking his head.

"You need to find out about Adika to see what's going on with her. Something is not right with her. She survived getting fucked and bitten by a wolf; that should've sent up a red flag," I said to Izra and everyone else agreed.

Another busty stripper came into our section. She sat on my lap playing with my necklace. "Would you like a private show, handsome?" she asked me, feeling on my chest. She wanted me to have her.

"Nah, I'm good," I said to her. She was pretty but I was not interested.

She looked at me angrily. "Nobody turns down Caramel!" she snapped at me.

"It's a first time for everything! Now, get your ass off my lap before my woman smells your scent on me," I said to her. She called me a punk and a few other words that I ignored.

I checked in on Kanya—the last time I checked in on her she and Adika were on their way to the club. When I eased into her mind, all I heard was screaming and crying. She was calling my name and she sounded wounded.

"What's going on?" I asked inside her head, standing up.

"We are being ambushed! It's nine of them!" Kanya screamed back.

"I need to get to Kanya!" I told the pack, rushing out of the club. I ran into the nearest woods bursting out of my clothes. Bushes ruffled behind me then I smelled my brothers. I took off running full speed as they ran behind me growling.

When I arrived at Kanya's location, I could not believe my eyes. Xavier was tossing her around like a pillow. I charged into him, slamming him into a car, tipping it over with all of my strength. Xavier got up then shook himself off. He paced back and forth taunting me for a battle. We charged into each other at the same time. I bit his neck then he yelped in pain. Amadi, Elle and Izra were fighting the other wolves, along with a witch and a large cat. I clawed at him until his mane was open and bloody, revealing flesh. His wounds closed up with every bite and slash I gave him. We fought, tumbling around in the parking lot. I tossed Xavier in the air; he came down with a loud thud. I growled then pounced on him, shaking him down as his blood ran from his body. The more blood he lost, the slower he healed. Xavier took something to make him stronger. I felt some teeth pierce through my neck as another wolf tried to fight me off of Xavier. It was his pack brother, Aki attack-ing me. Another one charged into me, biting the other side of my neck as they tried to pull me apart. Kanya tried to in-vade but she was slung across the parking lot into a light pole by Aki. I felt her pain and every bone that broke in her body. Three wolves were on me biting at my neck, tearing open my flesh. I grabbed one by the leg slinging him into a tree. There were only two on me. My wounds closed up and my heart beat faster as I felt my teeth grow longer and sharper.

Xavier no longer had a hold on me. I shook him off charging into Aki. I ripped opened Aki's throat and he fell onto the ground. I chewed into his flesh until I got down to the bone in his neck, biting into it…breaking it. The only way to kill an immortal is to sever their head from their body. Blood dripped from my mouth as I walked towards Xavier. He backed up then took off running with the other wolves following behind him. Two of his wolves were ly-ing in the parking lot dead. I ran over to Kanya, her body was wrapped up in the witch's dreads as the witch chanted. The cat licked Kanya's face nudging her head to wake her up.

"I'm healing her," the witch said. I realized the witch was Keora. I stared at Kanya as she slightly started moving. I could tell she was still sore. She broke her shoulder and hind legs when she went sailing into the light pole. People started coming out of the club; we disappeared into the woods with Keora and the cat following us.

When I entered the house, Kanya and I shifted back as we reached the hallway by our room. She limped into the room heading to the closet to get some clothes. I put on a pair of sweatpants. We had not said a word to each other. I was pissed at her again!

SOUL Publications

"I know that you're mad at me!" she said.

"You could've been killed! I keep telling you that there is trouble following you! I just wish your hard-headed ass would actually listen!" I said to her.

"You want me to remain in the house?" she asked me.

"Yes, that you will do! You will not leave this damn house unless I am with you! How about that? I been trying to give you freedom but now all of that shit is out the window! You are not leaving this house until I say so! There is nothing wrong with being submissive to your Alpha! From this day forward, you will learn how to be!" I shouted at her.

"Stop yelling at me!" she cried. I always forgot that Kanya feared me when I got upset but I could not help but to be angry.

"Stop making stupid fucking decisions then! This is the second time you have gotten hurt for not listening to me! I need to check up on my brothers to make sure they aren't injured because of you!" I said to her. I slammed the door after I left the room; the door came off the hinges.

When I walked into the living room, Keora was sitting on the floor Indian-style chanting and sprinkling dust on the floor. Amadi, Izra and Elle had wounds but they were minor. The black cat sat up in the corner by the doorway like an Egyptian Mau statue. It almost looked fake until it started licking the blood off its paws.

"I wish you three would put some clothes on!" Keora said to Amadi, Elle, and Izra as they walked around naked.

"Why would I do that, beautiful? This dick is a master-piece!" Izra flirted with Keora. The cat leaped on him.

"Get this damn cat off of me! I hate cats! Get it off!" Izra yelled as his body started to shift.

The cat jumped off him then shifted into woman form and she was naked! When she turned around it was Adika.

"I marked a damn cat! A fucking feline? I knew I should not have eaten the neighbor's cat years ago! That old lady was looking for Percy for two years!" Izra said.

Adika spun around then shifted into a Gorilla. She stood up then beat on her chest. "Oh, hell nawl'! What the hell is this shit? What kind of shifter is this? I fucked Cesar from Planet of the Apes?" Izra asked, getting angrier.

"She is my sister! She shifts into any animal she wants but she prefers the Mau. I can shift into any human I want, too!" Keora said, shifting into a naked Izra.

"What is going on in here and why is there so much yelling?" Kofi asked, coming into the room.

"Why are there two naked Izra's standing in the middle of the floor? And what the hell is a Gorilla doing in here?" Kofi asked everyone.

"You better stay your ass like that, Adika! You better not shift back naked!" Izra said, walking out of the room with Adika.

"I saw a lot of crazy shit tonight! I'm going to sleep!" Elle said and Amadi agreed. They walked out of the room and Kofi looked at me waiting for answers.

"It's me, Kofi!" Keora said, shifting back to herself. Kofi smiled then hugged her.

"The gorilla is Adika? So, she is the one that had Izra all hung up? What a small world!" Kofi said laughing.

"Care to explain!" I said to him.

"Your mother created those two thousands of years ago. They are from magic! They are like your sisters in a way!" Kofi laughed.

"Everyone knows my damn mother and father except for me? This is some bullshit! I need to see their faces!" I spat.

Kanya walked into the living room with a sad face. Kofi was ready to hug her but I stopped him.

"She doesn't need to be babied up! She needs to think about how much she jeopardizes not only her life but the rest of the pack's lives!" I said to him then he backed away from her.

"Well, I'm done here. I only followed to make sure everyone was okay. When Adika finishes fucking Izra, tell her that I went home," Keora said to us disappearing.

"Witches are very complicated women," Kofi laughed.

"Tomorrow we will talk about your parents because I think it's time you meet them, too. They have more answers for you than anyone else including myself," Kofi said, walking out of the room. It was just Kanya and I in the living room.

"You don't want to be with me?" Kanya asked me.

"We don't have a choice! We are permanent! I can never feel like I do not want to be with you. But right now, I don't have to be bothered with you at the moment," I said heading to our bedroom. I turned around and noticed that Kanya was going to the basement. "Upstairs, Kanya!" I called out to her. She rolled her eyes then marched up the spiral staircase.

When we walked down the hall, all we heard was moaning, screaming and glass breaking. There was a loud thump against the door with the sounds of furniture moving.

"Izra might kill her!" Kanya said to me.

"He's just being a wild animal!" I said to her.

SOUL Publications

Xavier

T he house was quiet as we mourned the loss of Aki. He was like a real brother to me. He and I had known each other since pups! Goon ripped him open dislocating his head from his spine. The horrific scene had been stuck inside my head. I could not eat or sleep. No one said anything to me, as I stayed hidden in my room. I had to think of a clever way to take Goon down. He got even stronger when Kanya was injured. I needed to figure out what could weaken him.

"Xavier, you have a visitor!" Lance said, knocking on my door.

"Tell them I'm not home!" I shouted.

"She said she really needs to talk to you!" Lance said.

"What's her name?" I asked Lance.

"Naobi!" he said. After I told Lance I would be right out, I quickly showered then got dressed in a T-shirt and a pair of jeans. I walked downstairs and into the guest room where Naobi sat with her smooth dark brown legs crossed. She held a basket on her lap. She smiled at me.

"We were worried about you at work. I heard you lost someone close to you. I brought you some brownies," she said.

"Thank you," I said. She stood up then straightened out her pencil skirt. It hugged her curves and slim waistline. Naobi was perfect! She had not one flaw.

"This is a very nice home you have here!" she said, looking around. I followed behind her closely so I could inhale the scent that poured from her neck. Her perfume was light and sweet!

"Well, I have to get going. I will see you at work tonight. Make sure you eat the brownies. I used my special recipe that is to die for," Naobi said, brushing the lent off my shoulder. Amilia barged into the house; she was still healing slowly. She was now able to walk around and become the pest she really was . She eyed Naobi then looked at me.

"You bring your whores to our home now?" Amilia screamed at me.

"She is the new bartender! If you would get off your lazy ass and go to work, you would know that! She brought me some brownies because she heard what happened to Aki!" I told Amilia.

"I'm sorry for my rudeness! My name is Amilia and you are?" Amilia asked Naobi.

"I'm Naobi! It is nice meeting you. Hopefully I will see you at the club," Naobi said, walking out of the door.

Amilia looked at me with her arms crossed.

"I want out of this pack," she said to me.

"So you and Dash can live happily ever after? I do not think so! We will mate as we planned! After you give me my pups, you will be free to go and do as you please!" I said, walking away from her.

I picked up the basket of brownies then took them into the kitchen. I poured a cold glass of milk then dipped the still warm gooey fudge brownie into the cup.

Later on that night…

I was in Club Fangz walking around making sure everything was going well. I started coughing and my nose started itching. Wolves don't get sick, so I wondered how I was having cold symptoms. I drank a glass of water but that only made the coughing worse. I went into the bathroom in my office to splash water on my face. I started coughing again then my tooth flew out into the sink.

"WHAT THE FUCK!" I shouted as I looked at my missing tooth. My hair started itching really badly and when I scratched my scalp, my hair fell out into the sink.

"NOOOOOOOOOOOO!" I yelled but it was silent because of the loud music.

"Xavier, come quick! We have a problem!" Joseph said, bursting into my office.

"What the hell happened to you?" Joseph asked, looking at the patches of hair missing from my head.

"I don't know! What's the problem?" I asked feeling stressed. A wolf never loses a tooth and we do not shed.

"Just come!" he said, running out of my office.

I followed behind him. When I got to the dance floor, there were big bats flying around the club. Everyone was yelling and screaming. Some people were knocked over onto the floor and stepped on. Naobi slowly walked back to the bar with the drink tray over her head. She was the only one who remained calm. My other bartenders ran out of the door with everyone else.

"I've never seen bats that big in my life!" Joseph said to me.

More bats burst through the club windows; the bats started biting me. Over fifty of them attacked me! I ran out the back door of the club then shifted. I knew this had something to do with those witch sisters! I grabbed a few bats off me, chewing them up then spitting them out. I was a bloody mess as they fed on me, they were vampire bats. I took off running through the woods to my home. Amilia screamed when I charged into the house. I shifted back then collapsed on the floor.

"What the hell happened to you?" she asked, turning me over.

"I'm cursed!" I said to her. Dash came out of the kitchen with just his pants on. He was sweaty and had claw marks going across his chest.

"You whore!" I said to Amilia.

"Amilia, get away from him!" Dash said to her and she obeyed him.

"You marked her? You son of a bitch!" I said to him then he chuckled.

"I marked her way before you even thought about mating with her. Why do you think you and her don't have a connection? Fuck you and this pack! Amilia and I are leaving. Amilia, go pack up your shit!" Dash said to her.

I charged into Dash and he was stronger than me. He slammed me down onto the floor and we went through the floor and ended up in the basement.

"The only reason you are Alpha is because your father made you Alpha! You don't have what it takes!" Dash said, kicking me in the face.

Dash was supposed to be Alpha after my father but my father thought it was only right that his son take his spot. Dash kicked me in the face again knocking out more of my teeth. Lance jumped down the hole in the floor then pulled us apart.

"I'm sick of this pack! Wolves have been killed because of this arrogant punk asshole! He is a coward! You stole from a witch putting this pack in jeopardy! Everything you have done was because of a woman who doesn't and will never belong to you!" Dash said to me.

"If you are leaving then I'm leaving with you!" Lance told Dash. Three of the new members came out of their rooms. They agreed to leave with Dash also. I could not lose my pack!

Amilia looked at me with a smirk on her face. "Looks like you need to get the hell out! This is no longer your pack!" she said, shifting into wolf form and so did the others. They growled at me backing me up into a corner.

I hurriedly got up then ran out of the house heading to my father's house. When I got there, he was putting suitcases in his trunk.

"Where are you going?" I asked him.

"When I sent you to those witches, I didn't send you there to steal from them! If a witch tells you no then that is what it means! You pissed off the gods! You are cursed, Xavier! Look at you! You look like an old man and wolves don't age!" he said to me.

"I lost my pack! What am I going to do?" I cried. I was losing everyone!

"You have to go away, Xavier! I told you more than once that you were upsetting the gods! You need to run away!" he told me.

"I'm your son! You can't abandon me!" I said to him. He closed the trunk.

"This is your mess, Xavier! I should have gone with my gut instinct! This is my entire fault!" he said then I backed away from him.

He let out a deep breath. "Amilia's father didn't want her with Dash because he said he wasn't good enough. He knew Dash had what it took to become Alpha. So, in exchange he gave us Club Fangz for you to be Alpha and take his daughter!" my father said.

"You set me up!" I said to him.

"I did what I did to make you Alpha! You are my son! I was a great Alpha and I wanted to prove to the other wolves you had what it took as well but you don't! Alphas are born from Alphas! It just hasn't come to you yet!" he said to me.

"How was I able to smell Kanya's scent?" I asked him.

"A spell. I bought a potion from the witch you stole from. The potion was to make you to an Alpha. I poured it on your steak a few years ago," he said sadly.

"You son of a bitch!" I said, charging into him. I tore into his throat dragging him across the ground. Old wolves do not shift as fast as younger wolves; I attacked while he was still in human form. I clamped down further until I felt his neck crush.

When I shifted back, I looked down at my dead father then cried. I did not mean to kill him! My stomach bubbled; I was going to be sick. I threw up big black water bugs; they kept coming out of my throat. I rolled around on the ground in my father's blood as the bugs crawled around inside my stomach. I threw up more of them along with blood. I was getting weak as I looked at my arms; they were very pale and blue. I weakly crawled away from my dad's house and into the woods. I had only one person in mind who could help me.

I weakly banged on the door holding my stomach. Sasha opened the door. "What the hell happened to you?" she asked, helping me off the floor.

"Xavier, you look dead! You are scaring me! Why are you naked?" she asked me.

"I was beat up and robbed!" I told her.

"They pulled your hair out, too?" she asked me.

"I need some water!" I told her. She hurriedly ran and got me some water. I was going to hide out here until I figured out how to get this curse off me. I laid on her couch guzzling the water. "I will pay you whatever you want me to! Just let me hide here," I told her. Sasha was not even aware that Aki was dead!

Kanya

*I*t had been four days since the fight outside of Xavier's club. I looked around the room and Goon was gone. He did not wake me up and I did not hear him leave. We had been sleeping next to each other but he was distant. He only rolled over and held me once during the night within those four days. When he realized what he was doing, he took his arm from around my waist. I had been aroused more times than I could count and he did not budge. He would not even touch me sexually. He was training his body to resist me, even though he wanted me. I headed to our bathroom then showered. I got dressed in lounge clothes to sit around and do absolutely nothing! Goon was serious when he said I could not leave the house. Tomorrow Goon and I were going to visit my parents. I was looking forward to that and tomorrow could not get here fast enough. I needed some air! Being the only female in the house was not fun at all. Oh, wait Adika was here but she was locked away in Izra's room. She had been in his room for days with the sounds of moaning and wood being scratched coming from the room.

Amadi said wolves were able to have sex for days! Izra came out for food then hurriedly went back to his room. The sounds of them screwing were getting me aroused at night! Goon even had a hard-on for the past couple of nights. I tried to please him with my mouth but he would not allow me. Not only was I restricted from the outside world, I was restricted from my man!

SOUL Publications

I knocked on Izra's door and moments later he opened it up with only basketball shorts on. He had scratches on his chest and hickeys all over his body. I covered my eyes.

"Can I talk to Adika for a second?" I asked him.

"She's sleep!" he said.
"Stop lying, Izra!" Adika called out to him.

He shut the door then whispered, "I thought you said you was going to shift into a Siberian husky while I fuck you!" My mouth dropped open even though Izra's blunt speaking did not surprise me.

"I will later!" Adika whispered back. Izra opened the door back up.

"So, you've been screwing Adika while she shifts into different animals?" I asked Izra then his handsome face lit up with excitement.

"Mannnnnn, that shit is beautiful! Last night she turned into a unicorn! I didn't know if I wanted to eat her and say fuck hunting or if I wanted to slide into her!" he said.

"Adika! Bring your ass out here! I'm not in the mood to entertain your crazy ass man!" I said to her. He slammed the door in my face. I could hear him tell Adika she had better not take no more than five minutes. Moments later, Adika walked out with a robe on and her hair was all over her head. She had bite marks on her neck and scratches on her chest.

"Seriously?" I asked her then she blushed.

"Izra's stamina is just amazing! I have been with thousands of men over the centuries and none of them made me submissive during sex!" she said to me.

"How old are you?" I asked her.

"I'm over a thousand years old. I don't age at all. I've never been a child. I was created from magic in the form I'm in now," she told me. I always wondered why Adika's looks had not changed since the ninth grade. She had a very youthful looking face; her body was the only thing that changed throughout the years.

"Great! Everyone around me is ancient!" I said laughing. She and I walked down the stairs.

Dayo came into the house dressed in his motorcycle gear. Dayo was very attractive! His skin was the color of the midnight sky. His eyes were hazel and his hair was a kinky-like texture. I still could not believe he was into men. Dayo had been spending a lot of time away from the house. He came in for a few hours then left right back out. I already knew it was because of me. He looked at Adika then sucked his teeth.

"Who are you?" he asked Adika.

"The woman that's dating Izra. Is that a problem?" Adika snapped back.

"So, I take it he found you off the streets, too? If I see another human woman, I am going to lose my mind!" he mumbled.

"I am not human!" I said to Dayo then he laughed.

"Oh, that's right! I forgot you are the prissy little non-hunting toy dog that everyone is going crazy about!" he said. I growled at him then he laughed.

"You got something you want to get off your chest?" Goon asked Dayo while coming from the basement.

"Nothing at all, bro!" Dayo said, smirking. He walked past us then up the stairs.

"WOW! Somethings seems odd with Dayo! I cannot put my finger on it yet and it's bothering me," Adika said.

"Now you see what I have been going through?" I asked Adika laughing.

"Heyyyy, Goon! Can't speak!" Adika teased him.

"Naw! You and Izra been keeping me up at night!" Goon smirked. I turned away from him because his slightest gestures made me get in the mood.

"You can look but don't touch until I say so!" his voice boomed inside my head while he and Adika held a conversation.

"I will be in the kitchen making some Mimosas and breakfast, Adika!" I said, walking away.

"I would like a steak!" Goon's voice said in my head.

"Fix it yourself!" I shouted. He and Adika laughed at me.

I prepared everyone's breakfast including Dayo's. Once I called everyone to the dinner table, just like a pack of wolves they came running. Adika and I ate breakfast at the small table in the kitchen.

"It feels so good to have another woman in the house! Even if just for a few days. Living with a bunch of arrogant men with insane appetites is not fun," I said to her.

"It's not that bad. Everyone is like a big family," Adika said.

"Izra isn't mad anymore?" I asked her.

"Nope! Once I turned into a unicorn, he was happy like a kid on Christmas! Izra is like a child at heart!" she smiled.

"He is the youngest out all of them. Maybe that's why he acts so darn ghetto at times," I laughed. After Adika and I had breakfast, we walked outside to the backyard.

"Kanya, are you sure you want to do this? Goon said not to leave the house," Adika said to me.

"You heard what Dayo said. He called me a non-hunting toy dog! I have never caught a deer by myself. I will be having pups soon, so I need to learn how to feed them. Therefore, Goon has to understand why I left the house. Besides, the gates go very far so I will still be on the property. I will be fine as long as I'm within the gates!" I told her. After I took my clothes off, I hurriedly shifted so no one could see me. Adika dropped her robe then shifted into a cheetah.

"Show off!" I said to myself.

"I heard that! Now, let's hunt!" she said, taking off full speed. I took off behind her, trying to catch up with her. I leaped up in a tree, jumping from tree to tree. Adika and I roamed around in the woods until we came across two deer.

I remembered the techniques Goon used when he hunted. He stalked the animal first then slowly crept up on it without making a sound. Adika watched me as I crept behind the bigger deer; he was huge. His antlers stretched out, looking like two small trees on top of his head. Deer antlers can be dangerous. Amadi caught one a few weeks ago and it tore up his stomach. I steadied myself until I got a clear view of its neck. He was eating grass. I charged into him sinking my teeth into its neck. The other deer tried to take off but Adika pounced on it. I wrestled the huge deer to the ground; he was very heavy and strong! I locked my jaws around his neck as he thrashed around almost knocking me off him. My nails dug into him to get a firm hold. His breathing weakened, I shook him by the neck snapping it. Adika and I dragged our kill back to the house. I was glad it was not too far! The deer was almost bigger than I was! The guys were waiting for us in wolf form back at the house. I was sure Goon read my mind and knew what I was doing. They were ready to eat even though they just ate a big breakfast! Goon walked towards me in his menacing black wolf form. He was beautiful in the daytime when you could see all of him. At night, his eyes were the only thing you could see because everything else blended into the night. His wolf mane was silky and bushy; the sculpted muscles in his shoulders, perfect. His entire structure was beautiful! When he got to me, he licked my face then nuzzled his head under mine. *"That's my girl!"* his voice said into my head. I licked his face back then charged into him. We rolled around in the grass wrestling and playfully biting each other.

"You still can't go anywhere!" Goon said.

The next day…

We pulled up in front of my parents' home. Goon looked down at my fake stomach that I had ordered online a week ago. "What?" I asked him.

"I'm still trying to figure out your meaning of that," he laughed.

"I will be having pups in three months, right? My parents have not seen me in three months. I can just say that I was already past my first trimester when they last saw me. This way, they won't be suspicious of me having babies so fast," I said to him.

"You really have a busy mind, Kanya," he laughed, getting out of the car.

When I got out, I stretched my body; my parents lived four hours away. They moved to New York a year ago. I talk to them almost every day and could not wait to see them. I rang the doorbell nervously; Goon looked at me with a worried look on his face.

"What's the matter?" I asked, rubbing his back.

"What am I supposed to say?" he asked then I blushed. Goon did not fear anything but witnessing him showing fear in meeting my parents was bringing out another side of him.

"Just be yourself. They are easy to talk to. A bit nosey but you will manage," I said to him.

"Are they nosey like you?" he asked me with a serious look on his face.

"Really, Goon! I'm not nosey!" I said then he smirked, kissing my lips.

"It is okay, baby," he chuckled.

Moments later, the door opened and it was my mother. She was a thick heavy woman. My mother was very eccentric especially with her natural locks and heavy wooden jewelry.

"My babbyyyyyyy!" she said, hugging me. She held my face in her hands as she placed kisses all over my face.

"I missed you," I said to her.

"And who is this very handsome young man?" she asked me.

"My name is Akua and it's nice to finally meet you. Kanya did not tell me how beautiful you were. I see where she gets her unique looks from," Goon said, shocking me. My mother blushed.

"Well, thank you! Kanya, I see you've got yourself a charmer!" she said, pulling us inside the house. The smell of vanilla candles burning filled up the brownstone.

"Can I get you two anything?" she asked us then her eyes landed on my stomach. She gasped then put her hands over her mouth.

SOUL Publications

"You are with child?" she asked me. Goon looked at me, waiting for me to lie to my mother. I wanted to pinch him for not helping me out.

"Yes, we will be expecting in three months. Kanya wanted it to be a surprise!" Goon finally said, rubbing my stomach.

My mother sat down on the couch. "Oh, my heavens! We are going to be grandparents! What are we having?" she asked us.

"I don't know yet! I don't want to find out until I go into labor," I told her. My father came down the stairs. He was shorter than my mother and very stubborn.

"Your father is a very small man! Maybe we should take him hunting with us! I've caught rabbits to snack on bigger than him," Goon said in my mind. I covered my mouth to keep from laughing. My father had a scowl on his face but it was the least bit menacing.

Goon stood up then held his hand out. "It's nice to meet you, Mr. Williamson," Goon said to him. My father looked at his hand then slowly shook it. I stood up then hugged my father.

"Hey, Daddy!" I said. He finally smiled hugging me back then kissing my cheek.

"Hey, pumpkin! Your mother and I been missing you! You picked up a lot of weight. Is that what I think it is?" he asked, touching my stomach.

"Yes, Akua and I are expecting in a few months," I said to him.

"But you are not married! You know this family doesn't have sex before marriage, Kanya," he scolded me. I saw a flash of anger in Goon's eyes.

"Cut it out, Jeffery! This is our only child and we will do anything to make her feel comfortable, including accepting this pregnancy," my mother spat.

"But, honey, Kanya isn't responsible yet and this young man looks like a thug!" he said. I touched Goon's hand and it was burning up; his beast wanted to come out.

"I'm fine, Kanya," Goon's voice came inside my head.

"Shut the fuck up, Jeffery!" my mother screamed at him.

"Maybe we should go. I did not drive all the way up here to feel unwanted. Akua and I are having a baby and we are happy.   Daddy, I love him and you have to get used to him because he and I are together forever," I said to him.

"Okay, let's just talk over dinner," my father said to us.

My parents walked out of the living room. I turned around and noticed Goon's facial expression. As long as I had known him, I had never witnessed him sad and unsure. I stood up on my tippy-toes, hugging him.

"What's the matter?" I asked him.

"They love you, Kanya. I do not want to take you away from them. This is what you are used to. Living in the house with a bunch of wolves isn't what's fair to you," he said, sounding like he was breaking up with me. If Goon walked out of my life, I think I would emotionally die!

A tear slid down my cheek. "Did you not see the pain I went through when those markings etched across my back? You are stuck with me! You are my life! I love you," I said to him. He kissed my lips.

"I know you do. I love you, too," he said, finally telling me. Hearing him say those words warmed my heart.

"I want to bite you right now," I said then he licked his lips.

"Oh, word?" he asked me then I laughed because of how much he sounded like a modern-day hood boy.

Goon and I joined my parents at the dinner table. My mother made rotisserie chicken, sweet potatoes and broccoli with freshly made buttered biscuits. Goon stared at his plate trying to figure out what he was going to eat first; he did not eat chicken.

"What's the matter, Akua? You don't like chicken?" my mother asked him.

"He is allergic. Goon can only eat red meat and vegetables. His stomach gets very sensitive, if you know what I mean," I whispered to my mother.

"Oh, okay. Eat what you want, honey," my mother said to Goon.

"So, where are you from Akua?" my father asked him.

"I'm from Africa, Egypt to be exact," Goon answered.

"I have some family that migrated from Egypt to West Africa ages ago. There was even this folklore tale about a witch turning a man into a wolf. The villages heard rumors about the witch and ended up going to see her. They wanted to live for eternity so she turned them into animal shifters. My grandmother used to tell me stories about it. She also told me that we have jackal blood and every thousand years, a jackal is born into our family. I love the stories about ancient Egypt!" my mother said. If only she knew how real those stories were.

"What do you do for a living?" my father asked Goon.

"He is a meat butcher," I answered for him.

"That's a good one!" he said in my head then laughed.

"How old are you? You don't look much older than Kanya," my mother said to him.

"I'm twenty-four," he answered her. After dinner, my father warmed up to Goon while my mother and I cleaned the kitchen. Goon even laughed at his corny jokes.

"You seem very happy. My only child is growing up," she said with teary eyes.

"Don't cry, Mama," I said, hugging her.

"I can't believe you left home and got your own life. If I could I would keep you here," she sniffled.

"I'm growing up," I laughed.

"I know that. Just make sure you visit more and bring my grandbaby to see us every chance you get. Or if it isn't too much we can always come to see you," she said.

Afterwards, I kissed my parents goodbye and promised to call them as soon as I got back in the house. Goon gave my mother a hug and my father a handshake before we left. When we got back in the car, I was exhausted.

"You sure you don't have any real pups in there? You been tired all day," Goon said to me.

"That's because this stomach is heavy," I said, taking it off.

"When the pups get older we will have to tell your parents what you really are. Your mother knows the story, she just doesn't know it exists," Goon said. I did not want to tell my parents at all. That would mess up their heads, might even set them crazy.

I stared at Goon's handsome face and my thoughts were spiraling out of my head. I wanted him badly! I hated going in heat! It always snuck up on me causing that uncontrollable throbbing between my legs. I pulled my pants and my panties off while Goon drove. He sniffed the air then growled.

"Kanya, if I shift while I'm driving that wouldn't be too good. That will set these people crazy seeing a big black ass wolf behind a steering wheel!" Goon said.

His hard-on was pressed against his jeans, it grew down his leg. I unzipped his pants then ripped the rest of the material along with his boxer-briefs off. I held his large member in my hand kissing the tip of it.

SOUL Publications

"OH SHIT!" Goon hollered out. I took him down my throat massaging his testicles. I slurped, licked, and slobbered all over him. He swerved the car off the road. "UMMMMM!" he moaned.

"FUCK!" he growled as my head went up and down, jerking him off in a faster motion. I slipped my fingers between my slit, as my essence splashed on the leather seats. Thoughts of Goon pinning me down thrusting in and out of me caused me to suck him faster; my fingers were dripping from my wet sex. My legs trembled as I climaxed.

"I'm about to explode!" Goon hollered out. His dick was harder and his veins bulged out; the tip of his head swelled then he exploded inside my mouth in the back of my throat.

He slammed on the brakes. I sat up and looked around at our surroundings. We were under a dark overpass. There were not any cars driving past.

"Get out!" Goon said, opening his door. I hurriedly got out then sat on the hood of the car. Goon spread my legs then pulled me down into him. His dick pierced through my opening causing my screams to echo. He ripped off my shirt and bra, capturing my hardened nipples into his warm mouth.

"Go deeper!" I screamed, dripping on the hood. I wanted him deep, long and hard. He held my legs up pushing more of his girth inside of my tight hole. I dug my nails into his forearms while he moved in and out of me.

"Bite me!" I screamed. I wanted him to give me that euphoric pain that brings me pleasure and intense orgasms.

SOUL Publications

Goon's canines expanded from his gums. His nails sharpened as he licked my neck then slowly sank his teeth into me. My legs shook then my body convulsed; my eyes rolled into my head as his bite traveled through my veins. I ripped open his shirt then kissed his toned chest. I brought his head closer to mine. I kissed his cheek then worked my way down to his shoulders. My teeth punctured through his skin, he howled. I threw my hips back into him faster and harder. My teeth went further into him making him fuck me harder.

"ARRGGHHHHHHHHHHH!" I screamed. He was buried so deep inside of me. I felt a warm fluid gush from between my legs as Goon hammered away, making my legs tremble. My head spun and I got dizzy as he filled me up with his semen.

"I guess we have to drive back home naked since our clothes are ripped up," I said then he laughed.

SOUL Publications

Goon

*K*anya laid asleep slightly snoring. I eased out of bed then went into the hallway. I whistled quietly and Elle, Amadi, and Izra came out of their rooms. Kofi opened the door; we shifted then took off running through the woods. We leaped over the gate and then headed in the direction of Xavier's house. I wanted to kill him and his whole pack off! I had to get it over with because Xavier didn't seem like he was going to stop his rampage; he always ended up just popping up. I waited for a week and now the wait was over!

I stood outside of his house then howled letting him know that I was challenging him. Elle, Amadi, and Izra paced back and forth with their tribal markings glowing in their fur. My nails sharpened when I smelled another wolf. Four wolves emerged from the back of the house. The door opened and a man stepped out who somewhat resembled a younger version of Kofi.

"I know who you are here for and he isn't here! Xavier is no longer apart of this pack and we will not fight his battles. However, if you cause harm, we will fight you. I am Dash, the new pack leader," he said.

"I think he is telling the truth, Goon," Elle said.

"I know! He is the alpha of this pack. Let's go!" I said to my pack. Izra lifted his leg up then released himself on the tree in front of their house. One of the wolves from the other pack growled at him ready to charge him. I jumped in

front of Izra then growled; the wolf backed away putting his head down.

"Stay off our territory and we will stay off yours!" Dash said to me. I turned around then headed home.

I paced back and forth in the basement thinking of where Xavier could be. I needed to get rid of him! I *wanted* to get rid of him!

"We tried his father's house. We found his father's body sprawled out in the grass with his neck dislocated," Elle said, coming down the basement stairs.

"We need to track his scent," I said to Elle.

Kanya came down the stairs rubbing her eyes and fixing her robe. "Why aren't you in bed? Is everything okay?" she asked me.

"I'm fine. Go back to sleep. I will be in bed shortly," I said, pacing back and forth.

"Why are you mad?" she asked.

"GO BACK TO FUCKING BED, KANYA!" I yelled at her though I did not mean to.

My beast was angry and he was trying to come out. He wanted Xavier more than I did. My beast and I were different and at times. I could not control him!

"Calm down," Elle said to me. I picked up the couch then hurled it into the wall.

"I need to find him! I won't sleep until Xavier is dead!" I said, pacing back and forth. Kanya walked up the stairs then slammed the basement door.

"You didn't have to yell at her like that, Goon! You need to have better control over your beast! You and he never agree on the same shit!" Elle said to me.

"I can't control him sometimes!" I said getting angry all over again.

Izra and Amadi came down the stairs. "We couldn't track Xavier's scent. I don't think he's around, he's hiding somewhere," Izra said.

I felt a ball of rage come over me. I let out a growl then swapped everything off the shelves. I was in both human and wolf form. I walked up the stairs to my bedroom. I turned the knob but it was locked. I banged on the door.

"Open the door!" I yelled at Kanya.

"Go away!" Kanya cried.

"Open this damn door, Kanya!" I kicked it open and it flew into the wall. She jumped up, petrified.

"Don't you lock me out! Ever!" I yelled at her.

"You're scaring me!" she cried but my beast did not care. He wanted Xavier; he wanted blood! He needed to kill. I picked Kanya up by her throat with my nails pricking her skin.

"LET HER GO!" Kofi yelled, charging into me. Elle, Amadi, and Izra helped him contain me.

Kanya ran out of the room. "Fight it, Goon! Fight it!" Kofi said to me. I breathed in and out slowly like Kofi had taught me over the years when my beast overpowered me. Every once in a while, I went through violent spells. When I was ten years old, I went back to the plantation killing everyone. I was a new wolf and I was craving the taste of human blood. I stayed in wolf form for a whole week because my wolf would not allow me to shift back to human form.

Izra patted my shoulders. "You good now?" he asked me. They stood me up.
"I'm fine," I said then they let me go.

I left the room searching for Kanya. I sniffed the air following her scent. I walked outside and there she was sitting on the steps. Her shoulders trembled as she cried.

"Leave me alone, Goon!" she said to me.

"I didn't mean it," I said.

"You were another wolf! Your eyes were not even the same! You usually look into my soul when you stare at me. Your eyes looked past me. You looked at me like I was nothing!" she cried.

I sat down next to her. "I can't control him sometimes! He does not forget even when I try to. He craves revenge and he won't let me rest until I get it," I told her.

WHAP! She slapped me in the face.

"Fuck you!" she said to me.

"I deserved that," I said. She stood up but I pulled her back down onto my lap. "Please, Kanya."

"Will you hurt our children?" she asked. That question pained me.

As I sat there, something wet fell from my eyes. I touched my face and the liquid was clear. It was a tear. I had not cried since I was a little boy stranded in the woods after my parents died.

Kanya looked at me then I turned away from her, wiping my face. She turned my face back around looking into my eyes. She threw her arms around me then squeezed me as she hugged me tightly. She did not say it but I read her mind. She forgave me but I did not feel worthy of it.

Two days later…

"Where are you taking me, old man?" I asked Kofi. We were walking in the woods. We were so far into the woods that it was starting to feel different.

"Remember that lake? That's where I found you," he said pointing.

"Oh, yeah. You gave me my first deer," I said, chuckling.

"I gave you your name, too! Did not think you would stick with it, though. I should've named Izra, Goon!" Kofi laughed. We continued to walk until we came across two uniquely shaped trees that stood side by side.

"If you look closely, those two trees are shaped like gates," he said. I stared at it and the trees did resembled gates. Kofi picked up a rock, throwing it between the trees. The rock bounced back.

"That is the gate to the world I come from and the world your parents live in. It opens every full moon," he said.

"Why are we here?" I asked him.

"Someone wants to see you," he said, blowing into a small gold horn that looked like a whistle. He blew into it three times then a bolt of lightning formed between the trees. I stepped back and watched on. A giant black wolf with a gold emblem around its neck appeared. His beast was twice the size of mine; he was massive in size! Almost the height of an elephant.

"What the fuck is that?" I asked Kofi, ready to shift just in case we were in danger.

"That's your father, Ammon," Kofi laughed. Ammon's teeth were gold and so were his claws. Kofi dropped down then bowed to him. The wolf disappeared; in its place stood a man that resembled me. He was dressed like an Egyptian warrior. He held a long, gold stick with jewels decorated around it in his hand.

"Come, my son! Let me see you!" his voice called out to me. I looked at Kofi; he nodded his head, telling me to go. I walked towards my father; he dropped his stick then pulled me into him squeezing me tightly.

"I get to finally touch you," he said to me. I did not know what to do or say. I had glimpses of him in my visions but I did not remember him.

"I will wait here," Kofi said to us. My father grabbed me then we disappeared. We ended up in some kind of temple with two large chairs sitting side by side. There was some kind of big crystal ball sitting on a gold and diamond table in the middle of the room.

"That ball holds all of your memories!" he said as I walked closer to it.

"Your mother and I watch you from here. Every time she cries for you, a marking forms on your body," he said.

"Kanya has those markings, too," I said, not understanding.

"Kanya is connected to you; every marking you have she will get eventually," he said.

"What about the rest of the pack? They have a few," I said.

"Theirs are different from yours. I marked them so they could protect you. Your pack is designed to protect you. They have markings of a warrior!" he said.

I looked into the ball and it was like a movie of my life. I was a little kid running through the sand. I had to be around five, tossing a few rocks into the Nile River. My mother came and got me because I was ready to tip over into the water.

Ammon laughed. "You kept your mother and I on our toes," he said. I continued to watch. I was about nine when Kofi was showing me how to make a bow and arrow. We were hunting lions for their fur.

"Kofi has always been around?" I asked him.

"Yes, Kofi is my good friend. We are like you and Izra," Ammon said. I saw one vision where Keora and I were being intimate in the grass. I looked to be around sixteen.

"How is that possible?" I asked him.

"Keora was in love with you but unfortunately the prophecy didn't see it that way. Every time a woman fell in love with you, we had to reincarnate you until Kanya came along. It was our only way to keep the prophecy going. Egyptians plan everything from birth; they have visions of the future. Kanya was in that future but we knew it would be years before she came along. So we recycled your life until then," my father said to me.

"This is too much," I said.

"I know, son! You've been reincarnated over three hundred times," he said to me.

"I don't remember any of this!"

"Kanya is the woman who you are destined to be with. No more lost memories and recycled lives," he said as I stared at the globe-like ball. It was another memory of Keora and me. I gave her a piece of jewelry and her smile lit up her face. "That's why she loves jewelry so much," I said, watching us.

Ammon laughed. "Keora was a bit of a handful. You met her in your fiftieth life. She was very heartbroken when we reincarnated you, erasing your memory," he said to me.

I touched the ball then my memories started flashing in my head. I got a glimpse of all my lives; I pulled my hand away from it.

"Follow me. I'm going to show you my world. We have to hurry because I do not want you to be stuck here until the next full moon when you and Kanya are supposed to mate," my father said. He pushed open the stonewall and I could hear Egyptian music playing. This was like the visions I had been having.

"It looks like home," I said. When we walked outside, the thick wavy sand surrounded us. The water was crystal blue and it sparkled underneath the sunlight. It looked like small diamonds were floating around in the water.

"You will live here thousands of years from now. We do not get old then die. Once we live for thousands of years, we come here. The Earth isn't big enough for a lot of immortals to walk around," my father said to me.

"Where is my mother?" I asked him.

"On Earth! She casted a spell sending her back to Earth to protect you," he said.

"From who?" I asked him.

"Xavier! I told her you would handle it but your mother has always been protective over you!" he said.

After he and I talked and walked around, it was time for me to head back. He pointed his stick up to the sky and a tornado-like wind headed towards me.

"I will see you in a few months when Kanya gives birth. Take care, son," he said to me. The wind picked me up then I disappeared. I came crashing down on the muddy ground in the woods.

Kofi was still waiting for me when I got back.

"It's a beautiful world, isn't it? I can't wait till I go back," he said, patting my back.

"You knew about Keora and me?" I asked him.

"Yes, but they were all memories. We were not allowed to share them with you. You had to find out on your own and now that you saw them, they can be discussed," he said. We headed on a long journey back home.

"Where did you and Kofi go? You've been gone all day!" Kanya said, sitting on my back massaging it. Her small hands felt like magic.

"I met my father," I told her.

"WHAT! And you are just now telling me? What happened? What's he like? Is he big and mean like you? Or is he like a spirit?" she asked me.

"His wolf is bigger than mine and no he isn't mean! His personality is like Kofi's. I was surprised myself," I told her.

"Did you find out everything you needed to know about yourself?" she asked me.

"Yeah, I did," I answered her.

"Why did you tense up when I asked you that? Are you keeping something from me?" Kanya asked me.

"Keora and I were intimate in my past life. She was in love with me. I didn't have that memory but she still has hers. She was forbidden from telling me so I never knew," I told Kanya.

"That bitch!" Kanya spat, getting off my back.

"What's the matter with you?" I asked her.

"I kind of bragged to her and Adika about our love making and she already knows what it's like to feel you inside of her!" She paced back and forth.

"I saw the vision but I don't remember nothing intimate with her. I don't even look at her that way. She is just a friend of ours. Are you mad?" I asked Kanya, getting up to hug her.

"No, I'm not. I am just jealous because I know her. She even healed me. I want to know if she still loves you," Kanya said worried.

"It's all about us, Kanya. If it were meant for me to be with her then she and I would be! My soul has been born repeatedly, just so I could be with you! I feel nothing for another woman!" I insured her.

She kissed my lips. "You are very smooth with your words!" she said, dropping her robe. The light from the fireplace illuminated her skin.

"I want to show you something!" she said to me. I dropped my sweatpants standing in front of her naked.

Kanya crawled up the wall onto the ceiling. She turned her body around with her back to the ceiling. Her wetness dripped, splashing onto the hardwood floors. I leaped onto the wall joining her. Her loud gasp blew out the fire in the fireplace when I entered her. In two weeks, Kanya and I would be ready to mate.

A week later…

Kanya stood in the kitchen humming and dancing as she cooked dinner. She was preparing Thanksgiving dinner, she even made a turkey. I didn't understand how she could still tolerate eating that kind of meat. The smell of it made my stomach turn. Nevertheless, I still wanted Kanya to enjoy her life doing the things she was used to doing. When Kanya was happy so was I; I felt everything that she did.

"Damn, that turkey stinks!" Izra said, causing us to laugh.

"Would you shut the hell up?" Kanya popped him with a wooden spoon. Kofi laughed then shook his head.

"I think it smells quite interesting," Kofi said. Amadi and Elle were butchering a baby cow. Dayo was stuck in his room not wanting to be bothered which had been the norm lately.

"We're here!" Adika sang, walking into the kitchen with Keora. Keora looked at me then smiled shyly. I looked at Kanya and she was looking at me.

"Did this bitch just smile at my man?" Kanya asked herself as she chopped the potatoes. Keora chuckled, reading Kanya's mind.

"Stop it!" I boomed inside of Keora's head.

"I can sense that you have your memory back," Keora's voice echoed inside my head.

"I saw a vision of us but it wasn't a memory. I don't remember anything that happened between us! Now, be respectful. Kanya knows everything," I said to her. Keora rolled her eyes. Adika and Kanya chatted away like always. I could sense that Adika knew nothing about Keora and me. I walked out of the kitchen with Izra following behind me.

"You fucked Keora?" Izra asked, getting straight to the point.

"Yeah, years ago. How do you know?" I asked him.

"I peeped how Kanya and Keora was looking at you! You dirty dog you!" Izra mocked.

"I'm glad I learned how to block you out of my mind. You are a pest," I laughed at him.

"I'm ready to go around the back of the house to smoke. That shit Kanya is cooking got the kitchen smelling foul and it is bothering me. Are you coming?" Izra asked me.

"Hell yeah," I laughed. Izra and I kicked it around the back of the house. Moments later, the sliding doors opened and it was Keora. "Awww, shit!" Izra said, getting up.

"Where are you going?" I asked him, not wanting to be alone with her.

"Kanya is a feisty little puppy! She bit the hell out of my ankles! I will have no parts of this shit! In human language, 'Nigga, you on your own!' Holla at me lata!" Izra said, hurriedly walking into the house.

I stood up ready to walk back inside, but Keora put a stonewall up over the sliding doors with a snap of her fingers.

"I think it's time we had a talk. I've waited years for you to see the memory of us," Keora said to me.

"What is there to talk about?" I asked her.

"I loved you! I still do. Do you know how hard it is for me to see you with another woman? I do not care about a prophecy, Goon. What you and I shared was real. The love we made brought tears to my eyes. I can still feel your powerful strokes when I close my eyes," she said sadly.

"I don't remember, Keora," I said to her.

"You marked me!" she screamed, making the wind whistle and the trees blow.

"I've never marked another woman," I said to her then she laughed.

"Oh, yes you did. You marked me. We did not mate but you marked me. I can still feel you. I can smell you. I've been pretending to make the gods happy but I am tired of it! I am not pretending anymore! Kanya is a sweet girl but she isn't good enough for you," Keora said. She walked over to me then shifted into her witch form, her long dreaded hair covering her breasts. She moved the hair from her left breast and there was a bite mark. "I refuse to close it up," she said to me.

"I don't feel nothing for you, Keora! I do not remember you! I saw it but it was just a vision. I had no feelings!" I said to her. Black tears slid out of her eyes burning her face.

"It hurts!" she screamed. Once her tears disappeared, the burned skin cleared up. She spun around then disappeared into the night air. The stonewall over the sliding doors disappeared, and Kanya was standing there looking at me. How was I supposed to tell her I marked another woman?

I opened up the door. "So, what happened?" she asked me.

"Nothing," I said walking away from her.

"You are lying!" she shouted at me.

"I have a lot on my mind, Kanya!" I told her.

"Me, too, but you are already tuned in. I can't get into your head but I bet Keora can," she said following behind me.

"She is a witch! They can get into anyone's head that they please!" I said to her. I went down into the basement to get my thoughts together. Kanya continued to follow me.

"You were just outside with her with the doors blocked! You two didn't talk about nothing?" she asked me.

"She still loves me. But we already talked about that," I said to her.

"Witch or not, that bitch is bold. She comes to my home and flirts with my damn man! And your ass is being secretive!" Kanya yelled at me.

"What is this attitude?" I asked her. No woman had ever expressed herself to me the way Kanya did.

"It's called, when a black woman is pissed off! You are used to those damn magical creatures, submissive fe-males, and any other immortal being that you have fucked! This is the world we now live in! What you and she did was disrespectful! In my face at that!" she screamed with her eyes turning gold.

"Calm down!" I said to her. She charged into me claw-ing at my face and biting me. My beast tried to come up but I had to control him. He would go into defense mode and probably kill Kanya. Her sharped teeth pierced through my skin and her nails scratched my face. She was attacking me still in her human form. I pushed her off me then she charged into me again, pushing me out of the window. The glass cut into my skin when I landed on the grass. She shifted into her beast, leaping out of the window; she paced back and forth in the grass growling. Her beast was getting stronger and more powerful. She was becoming mine; she and I shared everything!

A growl slipped from my throat then I shifted. I stood firm and tall ordering her to back down but she would not.

She paced back and forth challenging me to fight even though she knew I was capable of killing her. All of a sudden, she took off running in the opposite direction. I chased behind her but she was faster. She jumped into a tree and leaped from tree to tree until she disappeared. I invaded her mind and she was angry with me.

"Come back!" I told her.

"I need to blow off some steam!" she replied.

Kanya had been gone for hours. I laid in bed wide-awake then then doorknob turned. Kanya walked in naked and bloody. I could smell the deer blood on her. The best way for a beast to blow steam is the taste of blood. She headed straight to the shower, and the steam fogged up the bathroom when I walked in behind her. She growled at me, so I stepped back out of the bathroom. After her shower, she got in bed with her pajamas on. She usually slept naked but now she was fully covered up. She laid at the far end of the bed, and when I reached out to her, she gave me a warning growl. I hurriedly scooted back; Kanya's teeth felt like knives! Usually I healed right away but now it took longer for my wounds to close. Kofi said that only our mates could inflict that much pain. Kanya was the only one who could possibly kill me. She snatched the covers towards her pulling them off me.

"Fuck this shit!" I said, mounting her.

"Get off of me!" She tried to wrestle me but I was stronger.

"Calm down!" I said, pinning her down.

After she tired herself out, she calmed down. I ripped off her pajamas, exposing her naked body. I pulled her into me, feeling the warmth from her body that made me sleep peacefully. I held onto her then covered us up. She snuggled into my chest growling at me.

"Hush that shit up, Kanya, it's bed time!" I said to her. I caressed her back until she drifted off into a peaceful sleep. I wrapped my arms tighter around her, swallowing her in my embrace. I would be sick without her!

Xavier

I'd been on Sasha's couch for a few weeks, fading away. I was frail as a skeleton. I was going to die and I did not have the energy to find a cure for my curse. I paid Sasha as agreed; she had been taking care of me. Someone knocked on her door; Sasha opened it up.

"Hey, I used to work for Xavier. I wanted to know if I could see him. It will only take a second," the familiar voice said.

"Let her in," I said weakly. Moments later, Naobi came in smirking at me. *How did she find me?* I thought.

"I'm sorry I didn't catch your name?" Sasha spat.

Naobi whispered something in Sasha's ear. Sasha dropped down to the floor with a loud thud. Her body was lifeless; Sasha's body started drying up like a raisin until she looked like an Egyptian mummy. Naobi laughed. "My dear, Xavier," she said to me.

"Who are you?" I asked. I tried to sit up but my body was too weak.

"How were those brownies?" she laughed.

"It was you! You cursed me!" I said to her.

"You know I take my son's life very seriously. I know he can handle himself but I just had to make this one personal," Naobi said, straddling me.

"Your son?"

"Yes, Goon is my son. What you were doing upset the gods! Your father warned you repeatedly and you laughed about it, not being cautious to his warnings! Well, I am here to collect your soul and send you to hell, where the demons can feed off you! They have been starving for quite some time now," she laughed. I tried to wiggle her off; she grabbed my face sucking my soul from my body and into her mouth, sending me into a dark place where I would live for eternity.

Kanya

G oon had been trying to explain himself to me, letting me know that he and Keora had nothing together. I believed him but it did upset me that she had a connection to him and sneakily flaunted it in my face. Adika was not aware of Goon and Keora when I told her about it, she was stunned. Adika stated that Keora was very secretive and often blocked her from her mind. The full moon was tomorrow night and I was nervous about it. Goon and I would become a family in just a few months.

"Get dressed!" Goon said, bursting into the room.

"I don't feel like it," I said to him. The mating was heavily on my mind.

"Come on, let's get some fresh air. It's a beautiful day," he said smiling.

"Why are you so happy?" I asked him giggling.

"Tomorrow night is going to be special for us. I'm going to fatten up your stomach," he said. He picked me up throwing me over his shoulder.

POP! He gave my ass a hard spanking.

"Ouch!" I said. He rubbed where he spanked me then kissed the side of my buttock. He took me into the bathroom then sat me down on the counter. He ran my bath water dropping some oil into the water that smelled heavenly.

"Amadi must have just made that one. It smells different from his other oils," I said.

"Yes, it does smell good," he said. Goon took off his clothes then grabbed us some towels from the bathroom closet. His dick smacked against his muscled legs with each stride he took. I hungrily licked my lips. He carried me into the tub then sat me down on the edge.

"It still amazes me how strong you are. You pick me up like a feather," I said to him.

"I'm supposed to," he said, opening my legs. He poured oil on my feet then massaged them. I threw my head back as his strong hands traveled up my legs. He kissed my inner thighs, working his way up to my throbbing pussy. He gently bit my inner thigh causing me to moan. He inhaled my scent, nuzzling his nose into me sniffing me. I bit my bottom lip when his warm wet tongue entered me.

"OOOOHHHHHHH!" I moaned, wrapping my legs around his neck. His head thrashed around as he licked, sucked, and slurped me. I slowly humped his face digging my nails into his shoulder as his tongue went in and out of me.

"UMMMMMMMMMM!" he moaned devouring my essence. He pinched my nipple then massaged my breast while his tongue went deeper into me, licking my sensitive spot that made me squirt. He pinned my legs up, stuffing his face into me. I looked down at him and his eyes were staring into mine, while his tongue flickered feistily across my swollen pink bud. He sucked on my hole slurping up the mess I spilled. Goon licked me dry from my pussy to my rear end after my essence flooded out. After he was done, he pulled me into the tub with him. I almost went under water because my body was still experiencing an orgasmic high. I could understand Keora's pain, but he was all mine! Every bone, limb and hair on his body!

"Whoa! Don't drown!" He pulled me up, making me blush from embarrassment.

After we were done, we got dressed and headed out to spend the day together. Goon was relaxed, smiling and laughing a lot. You could not tell that he had a beast hidden inside him. I wished he was like this all the time but he wasn't. His beast was what defined him, and I loved every bit of it even when it frightened me.

We spent hours in the mall and anything my heart desired Goon purchased for me. I still could not believe how much money the pack had; it was almost as if it was an endless amount. They had collected many valuable items over the centuries that were worth millions. Goon carried all of my bags, not allowing me to carry one. I still had a difficult time letting him do everything but he was my Alpha. When we got home the house was quiet. I changed into my comfortable clothes then headed to the kitchen for my chocolate milk.

Dayo was in the kitchen, drinking a pitcher of water. He must have just gotten back from hunting. I rolled my eyes at him then he chuckled.

"Your attitude bores me," he said.

"And your feminine ways bore me and they don't compete with mine. Just face it. You cannot have what I have," I said to him.

"Even beasts give into temptation if the right one brings it out," he replied.

"Are you telling me that Goon will be in lust after your hairy wolf ass? You've got to be kidding me," I said, slamming the refrigerator door. I noticed something was off about my chocolate milk; it looked like it has been tampered with. Dayo eyed me as if he was waiting for me to drink it. I went to the sink and poured it out. I walked passed him, pushing him out of my way. I didn't know for sure if he messed around with my milk but I wasn't going to chance finding out.

The next day (Full Moon) …

I woke up drenched in sweat as my pajamas and the covers stuck to my body. My body burned as if I had a high fever. My muscles ached and I was thirsty. My breasts were hard and extremely sore; I moaned out in pain.

"What is wrong with her?" Goon asked Kofi. Goon placed a cold rag on my head.

"Her body is getting her ready for pregnancy," Kofi said to Goon. A pain shot up my back through my spine. I burst into tears then another one came. Amadi burst into the room with a cup filled with hot water.

"Drink this, Kanya!" he said, giving me some type of nasty smelling herb.

"NO!" I yelled, knocking it out of his hand.

"You have to calm down!" Goon said.

"It feels like I'm having a horrible menstrual cycle! How in the hell am I'm supposed to mate, feeling like this?" I asked them in pain. My nails ripped up the sheets as another one came. "DAMN IT!" I yelled. It took my breath away as my body fell back onto the bed. My body temperature was getting hotter; I started tearing off my clothes. Kofi and Amadi covered their eyes, Goon tried to cover me back up. "I'm hot!" I said to him.

"Is that blood?" Goon asked me.

I looked between my legs and there was blood on the sheets. "What is wrong with me?" I cried.

"Your uterus is expanding for the baby. That way when he or she grows fast it will have enough room," Kofi said. Izra came in with cold wet towels. Goon snatched them from him.

"Cover your eyes next time!" Goon spat at Izra. Goon covered my body in the wet ice-cold towels, cooling me off. Elle came in with more towels; Goon wrapped me up in them. They were soothing and relaxing. Elle brought me a pitcher of ice-cold water. I guzzled the whole thing down and I was still thirsty. I felt like I had been running nonstop in the sun all day. Elle was taller than everyone in the pack. He stood at six-foot-five, his complexion was like caramel and he had hazel eyes that matched his wolf. Elle had an athletic build and looked to be only thirty years old. He re-sembled Ky-Mani Marley, even had locks in his hair.

"I love you guys," I said, feeling better.

"I told you she was crazy," Izra whispered to Goon.

"I heard that, jack-ass," I laughed. Everyone left the room all except for Goon. I drifted off into a peaceful sleep.

"UMMMMMM!" I moaned with a burning desire between my legs. My nipples stood up like two missiles. I sat up and all of a sudden, long braids with gold beads at the ends of them, fell down my face. There were clean sheets on the bed and candles were lit around our bedroom.

"Goon!" I called out to him. He appeared in human and wolf form. I looked out the window and it was a full moon. I must have slept all day. Goon's body was black and more chiseled; his stomach muscles more profound. His face was like a wolf's; he was also taller! I saw this form of him in my dreams. I reached up to touch his face; he bent down so that I could.

"Are you afraid?" he asked. It was an ancient deep voice with a heavy accent. I realized it was the same voice that was hunting me before I knew who he was. I looked down at my body and I was dressed in a thin, gold, sheer see-through sequined robed that dragged the ground. It hugged my body perfectly; my nails were pure gold. I went to look in the mirror and I almost did not recognize myself. My pupils were pure gold and my eye make-up was dark and heavy. It reminded me of Cleopatra, the ancient Egyptian goddess. I also had a thin gold band wrapped around my head.

"You are so beautiful!" Goon's voiced boomed inside my head. He stood towering over me by almost two feet. He was massive! I felt like a shrimp compared to him. His clawed hands caressed me up and down my body. His nails ran down the middle of my gown tearing it but it looked like he was unzipping it. He picked me up carrying me over

to the bed laying me down. His ancient form was what I had been craving in my dreams. His large, tall, muscled body was going to overpower me. I kissed his massive chest making him growl. He licked my breast gently causing my back to arch. My pussy throbbed like a heartbeat, my wetness flooded out of me dampening the sheets. My breathing sped up when Goon turned me over. Mating was not foreplay or love making. It was a battle of becoming one. Goon's heavy gold jewelry clanked together as he spread me apart. I arched my back, sticking my ass up higher to take his width. With this form being bigger than his human form, I knew his dick was bigger, too! He sniffed my essence causing it to run down my leg. My eyes watered as I waited for him to enter me. My body needed it! I could not wait any longer.

"Please, Goon! I need it! It hurts!" I cried as my pussy throbbed harder, causing my body to shutter.

He positioned his dick in front of my center; the head of it was huge! I panted like a dog in heat, waiting for him to penetrate my tight wet walls. He pushed his massive dick into me, causing me to scream. The windows flew open then the long curtains blew. He eased himself into me more.

"ARRGGHHHHHHHH!" My body trembled as I instantly had an orgasm. Sweat beads dripped from my breasts down my stomach when he gave me more of him. I dug my nails into the mattress, ripping a hole in it. He thrusted forward, entering my stomach. I craved him badly! I wanted him to go deeper and harder! He pulled out then slid all the way back in until my pussy made his dick disappear.

"AHHHHHHHHHHHHHHHH!" I moaned with tears running down my face. Every bone in my body felt like noodles. Goon held my arms behind my back with one hand with the other gripping my hip as he sped up, fucking me like the beast he is. Every thrust knocked the wind out of me making the room spin. I felt high off a drug; it felt like ten hands were caressing me, pleasing me all over.

SPLAT! SPLAT! The noise of his dick caving into my wetness echoed throughout the room. I arched my back more and was now lying face down into the mattress as he pummeled me. He growled and bit me, his clawing opening up my skin but all I felt was his massive size thrashing around inside me.

I threw my hips back into him, and the veins in his dick swelled up. My pussy slid up and down on him; I felt the pressure in my chest from his dick pushing my stomach up. I panted heavily.

"BITE ME! PLEASE, BITE ME!" I screamed.

Goon sank all of his teeth into my shoulder and that wonderful feeling took me over the edge. He pinned me down, placing his heavy body on top of me. He gripped my hips, fucking me harder and deeper. He growled, biting me again, causing me to scream. His dick punctured my spot then he got stuck inside of me, swelling up to twice his size in width. I stopped breathing as my body trembled. Goon let out a loud, hoarse, deep howl that shook the walls and the bed like an earthquake. The pictures fell onto the floors shattering. He howled again louder and deeper then I felt his wolf serum shoot into me, burning through my veins. My head felt like it was ready to burst, my body convulsed, as I experienced an orgasm so intense that I could not control my body as it trembled. My eyes rolled back into my head as his wolf serum continuously pumped into me, giving me intense orgasms. I could not breathe as I came repeatedly. His dick continued to swell, shooting liquid inside me. He bit me again, pumping more of it into me like a machine gun, causing my body to jerk each time. I felt like I was possessed, I could no longer handle it. Goon howled again louder than the first two and my ears were ringing from his deep hoarse howls. My stomach swelled slightly and Goon collapsed on top of me still inside me. I passed out...

The next morning, I woke up groggily. I looked around and our bedroom was a disaster. I got out of bed with my body aching and a pain between my legs. I looked down and gasped, my stomach was swollen. I looked to be around five months pregnant. Goon came into the room with a sad look on his face.

"What's the matter?" I asked him.

"We fell into a deep sleep after we mated! We have been sleeping for two days. I did not get a chance to see Kofi leave. My brothers said he tried to wake us up but we wouldn't budge," Goon said.

"We will see him again. I can feel it in my heart. Besides, he told me he's coming to visit when the portal opens up again," I said to him.

Goon rubbed my stomach then smirked, making me blush. "You took all of my wolf! I thought I killed you when you passed out but you went into a deep sleep," he said. He prepared my bath then helped me into the water.

"We are going to clean up the room while you bathe," Goon said, leaving the bathroom, shutting the door. I relaxed in the tub until I heard sweeping and loud laughter. Izra and Goon were arguing about something. I chuckled when Goon told Izra to go clean Adika's litter-box. Amadi and Elle roared in laughter.

I closed my eyes. *"Will Kanya eat deer meat or cow meat this morning?"* I heard Goon say.

"I take cow meat! Lots of it! Make sure it's bloody!" I said to him.

"You just heard my thoughts! Don't overdo it, Kanya. You are a bit nosey," he said then laughed. Once they were done cleaning up, I got out of the tub then walked into the shower to clean off. Moments later, I was dressed comfortably in a sweat suit and tennis shoes. I sat down at the dining room table; Goon came out of the kitchen with a meat platter stacked up almost to the ceiling.

My stomach growled when he sat the beautiful, fresh red meat in the middle of the table. I did not waste any time stuffing my face. Goon, Izra, Elle, and Amadi stared at me in shock as I growled biting into the thick steaks with blood dripping from my mouth. After I cleaned my plate off I was stuffed.

"That was for everybody, Kanya!" Goon said then laughed. I felt embarrassed but I could not help it.

"So, I'm guessing Kanya is having around four to five pups," Izra said.
"I'm having two. I can feel them moving around inside of me. I feel two separate heartbeats," I said, placing my

hand over my stomach. I felt little flutters and it tickled me. Goon sat down next to me rubbing my stomach.

"I can feel it, too!" he said to me smirking.

"If Izra and Adika mate, what do you think they will have?" Amadi asked us.

"Real fucking funny, Amadi! Don't get mad when I spray on your door again," Izra said.

"Spray?" I asked them.

"Izra doesn't have any home training. He likes to go anywhere he pleases," Goon said laughing.

"I'm just embracing my wild nature," Izra said.

"There is nothing wild about a dog fucking a cat!" Elle teased then he and Izra started wrestling each other. I laughed until I had tears in my eyes.

Two months later…

"UGGHHHHHHHHHHHHH! FUCKKKKKKKK! PULL THEM OUT!" I screamed as everyone stood in the room watching me go into labor. Elle took the place of a doctor. Adika placed a rag over my head. Goon paced back and forth not knowing what to do. He was upset that he could not ease my pain. Amadi and Izra looked on in horror.

"Push one more time, Kanya! I see the head!" Elle said. I pushed as hard as I could until I heard small whimpering.

"One more time, baby! There's another one!" Goon said, squeezing my hand. I squeezed his hand as hard as I could while I pushed the second one out. Elle cut their umbilical cords; Goon cleaned them off then handed them to me.

"They look human," I said with my eyes watering up.

"They are human until they turn ten. That's when they will shift for the first time," Goon said to me.

"The boys are beautiful," Adika said. The twins opened their eyes and a flash of blue flickered through them. They were going to be beasts like their father; they looked just like him. Everyone congratulated Goon and then left the room. They reached for my breasts, each pup latching on. I held them in both arms as they suckled away.

"They are going to be big and strong like their father! Look at them go, Kanya!" he smiled, kissing their foreheads.

"You think your parents are watching?" I asked Goon.

"I'm sure they are," he laughed. I was still curious about Goon's mother.

"My mother came into my dreams last night. She told me she will see me soon," Goon said. I kissed his lips; he wrapped his arms around the three of us. This is my new family; my complete pack.

"What are we naming them?" I asked Goon.

"Kanye and Akea, similar to our names," he replied.

SOUL Publications

"Those are African names, aren't they?" I asked him.

"Yup, from our roots!" he chuckled.

"I love it!" I said, kissing his lips.

Dayo

I was hidden away in a dark dungeon with only a few candles for light. I had been in this dark place for months now. My thoughts were blocked away from everyone; no one from the pack could reach me.

"It's time to eat!" a voice called out to me.

"Will you let me go?" I asked.

"Once my job is done, I will!" she said.

I met her at a club a few months ago. She was an ebony beauty with a lot of sex appeal. I went back to her place where she seduced me then put a spell on me after we were intimate.

Keora smiled wickedly at me. "Being you is very interesting! Sad that the pack thinks you are a wolf that's interested in Alpha males," she teased.

"You wicked bitch!" I charged into the cage that burned my skin to keep me from escaping.

"Well, let me be wicked, Dayo! You will stay here until I have everything I want!" Keora said to me.

"The gods are going to be upset," I told her then she laughed.

"Fuck the gods! They did not care about me when they took Goon away from me! They did not care one damn bit! All they were concerned about was that damn Kanya! Thanks to you giving into your beastly desires for fresh pussy, I am able to get close to the twin pups," she said to me.

"You'd better not!" I said, charging back into the cage again. She spun around then shifted into me.

"How do I look? You know, I'm also getting better at turning into your wolf! It took spell after spell for me to shift properly. All I need is your blood to become a warrior like the rest of them. Goon and Kanya both whipped my ass or should I say your ass?" she asked, laughing.

"Goon won't believe it! He will catch on to you! He knows that I would never fall in love with him. He is my fucking brother. Wolves don't lust after the same sex!" I said to her.

"Well, the images he saw when he thought I was sleeping as you tells him otherwise! Goon is all about brotherhood! He thinks you are in love with him and still has not kicked you out yet. I know his heart," she laughed.

"I'm going to get out of here! And when I do, I'm going to rip your fucking throat out! You crazy delusional bitch!" I charged into the cage again.

"You will never get out! No one knows that you are here! The gods do not even know! It took me years to cast a spell where your thoughts and visions cannot be traced by the gods or the pack," she said.

"You've been planning this?" I seethed.

SOUL Publications

"Yes, I have been! I want him back and I will do anything to get him," she said, leaving me in the dark dungeon.

I was a prisoner in hell! I needed to find a way to warn my pack! Keora had been practicing spells that could put everyone's lives in danger.

The End for now...

SOUL Publications